Someone is bound to get burned . . .

Meg Buchanan is determined to prove she didn't get the trainer job in Redmond, Oregon's rookie smokejumper class because of her family's long history as firefighters there—or out of pity. But if teaching one of her own brothers isn't challenging enough, Lance Roberts is in the new class of recruits. Once her brother's best friend, and her first, unrequited crush, he's also the son of the man responsible for her dad's death.

Lance is stunned to realize that this confident redhead is the stubborn girl he once dreamed about. There's no way he can fall for her now. He needs to focus all his attention on his training—and discovering the truth about the long-ago fire that killed both of their fathers. But as the undeniable heat between them threatens to ignite, someone attempts to put an end to Lance's amateur sleuthing—and his life

Visit us at www.kensingtonbooks.com

Books by Marnee Blake

Smokejumpers series
Tempt the Flames

Published by Kensington Publishing Corporation

Tempt the Flames

A Smokejumpers Novel

Marnee Blake

LYRICAL PRESS
Kensington Publishing Corp.
www.kensingtonbooks.com

Lyrical Press books are published by
Kensington Publishing Corp. 119 West 40th Street New York, NY 10018

All Kensington titles, imprints, and distributed lines are available at special quantity discounts for bulk purchases for sales promotion, premiums, fundraising, and educational or institutional use.

To the extent that the image or images on the cover of this book depict a person or persons, such person or persons are merely models, and are not intended to portray any character or characters featured in the book.

Special book excerpts or customized printings can also be created to fit specific needs. For details, write or phone the office of the Kensington Special Sales Manager:
Kensington Publishing Corp.
119 West 40th Street
New York, NY 10018
Attn. Special Sales Department. Phone: 1-800-221-2647.

First Electronic Edition: September 2018
eISBN-13: 978-1-5161-0768-1
eISBN-10: 1-5161-0768-3

First Print Edition: September 2018
ISBN-13: 978-1-5161-0771-1
ISBN-10: 1-5161-0771-3

Printed in the United States of America

To Terri Osburn and Jessica Ruddick, for always talking me off those ledges.

And to George… because.

Chapter 1

Driving from Bend to the smokejumper base in Redmond, Oregon, was like traveling back in time. It only took a half an hour, but the trip set Meg Buchanan back ten years.

As she pulled into the parking lot of Redmond Air Center, the tires of her Forerunner crunching on the dirt and gravel drive, she repeated the pep talk she'd been giving herself the entire ride.

She had the job. She was officially an assistant trainer and safety instructor for this year's Redmond smokejumper rookie training.

She wasn't a firefighter, but she was a physician's assistant with lots of practical medical knowledge. She was qualified. More importantly, she was a seasoned triathlete. She was in tiptop shape, and she definitely could run some rookies through their paces. Add her willingness to do the job for barely any money and her uncle's glowing recommendation, and she'd been approved.

That was her mantra. She could do this. She had the skills. She'd been approved.

She refused to accept that she'd been given this job because of her last name.

Sure, Will, her oldest brother, was an active Redmond smokejumper, and Uncle Joe was the base manager. Her middle brother, Hunter, would be in this year's rookie class. Together, they made a pretty impressive Buchanan family legacy at Redmond.

But, if she'd received preferential treatment, it was because her father's name—Jason Buchanan—rested on the memorial wall at the base, along with the other firefighters who'd given their lives in sacrifice to this job.

After shifting the truck into park, Meg dropped her hands into her lap and abandoned that train of thought. No use tempting the universe by spilling doubt and negative energy all over it. She had the experience, and she was going to give this job everything she had.

This was her chance.

She'd never been able to become a firefighter like her brothers. After hours of counseling, she couldn't overcome her paralyzing fear of fire. But, this? She could do this. These rookies were in for the training of their lives.

And she'd finally feel like she was honoring her birthright.

With a deep breath, she checked her reflection in the rearview mirror. She'd pulled her red hair into a low ponytail and applied light makeup. Dressed in tan slacks and a pale pink blouse, she looked more like she was seeing patients than reporting for a physical trainer position. She was more comfortable, though, professionally dressed, put together.

If things were orderly on the outside, the inside would follow. She'd learned that lesson years ago, after her father's death. Her mother had cried, and their home fell to pieces. When people showed up with food and condolences, the disaster in the house amplified how broken they were. Dishes in the sink, overflowing laundry baskets. Sleep eluded Meg those first nights, so she washed dishes, did laundry, and dusted until her body gave out. The next day, she'd cooked to fill the silence. The days stretched on, and no one ate unless they were reminded.

Eventually, though, the movements of normalcy made her feel more normal.

Fake it 'til you make it, her mom had joked. She'd never taken that advice, but it had worked for Meg. Pretend until the lie matched reality.

She exhaled slowly, pursing her lips. With shaking fingers, she smoothed her perfectly tidy hair once more, nodding at her reflection. She had this.

Snagging her wallet and phone off the passenger seat, she tossed them into her well-worn gym bag and zipped it up. Slinging it over her shoulder, she gripped the straps to her chest like a shield and opened the truck door.

Gravel bit into her ballet flats, but she ignored the discomfort. Around her, the parking lot was full of pickup trucks and Jeeps, a few larger SUVs and late-model sedans, and even an Econovan thrown in for good measure. The van had curtains. She wouldn't be surprised if its owner lived out of it.

There were a few guys unloading their cars, yanking duffel bags and equipment from trunks. Most of them were in their twenties and thirties. All of them were in amazing shape. The uniform seemed to be a mix of camo, Under Armor, and facial hair. A couple of the men paused to watch her walk by.

Maybe she should have put on her running clothes, some track pants. She looked as out of place in her business clothes as a peacock at a rhino tea party.

Her eyes straight forward, she hiked her bag higher on her shoulder and picked up her pace. As she approached the door, her uncle stepped out.

"Meggy." His smile, buried under a few days of beard growth, was as warm as always. Her shoulders relaxed in response. "You're early."

She stepped into his open arms. Uncle Joe gave the best hugs. "They pulled back on my hours last week in preparation for my time here. I finished earlier than expected today."

He leaned out of their embrace, scowling at her. "You're sure this won't affect your position with Dr. Colman, right? They'll let you return when training is over?"

She grinned at him. "I told you. Dr. Colman is happy that I'm helping. She's fine." It had taken a little sweet talking, playing up how good of a community outreach opportunity this was and promising to pick up shifts on the weekends while she was at the air center. Patrice Colman recognized a good deal when she saw it. She'd wanted to start opening on Saturdays for months, so she hadn't passed up this opportunity. But, Meg wasn't about to tell Uncle Joe that.

He patted her shoulder. "That's good, then. I'm not going to answer to your mom if this impacts your career."

Meg stiffened. "I'm twenty-five, Uncle Joe. I manage myself." Besides, they both knew her mother hadn't managed much of anything in years.

Joe nodded. "Right. Well, your brothers should be here soon. Do you want me to show you around?"

She laughed. "It's been a while, but I think I know where I'm going." She and her brothers had visited her father here often. Years ago, her mother would bring the smokejumpers cookies, muffins, whatever. She used to love to bake, and it gave her an excuse to see her husband. These days, the only time her mother's oven heated was for the Sunday dinners Meg cooked for them.

Meg scanned the exterior of the air center. "Place hasn't changed." Ten years later, but the air center looked the same. Behind the hangar, the airfield stretched across the open field. The Cascade Mountains filled the horizon. Here, without the multi-story buildings in Bend, the peaks were in full, majestic view.

"Why ruin a good thing?" He chuckled, wrapping an arm around her shoulder. "Come on. Let's get you settled."

As he guided her to the door, the rumble of an engine made her pause.

Either the Jeep that turned into the parking lot needed a new muffler or its owner wanted everyone to hear him coming. As it parked, everyone in the lot had stopped to look. Which meant this truck wasn't a regular fixture at the air center's lot.

She sniffed. Apparently, the diva of this year's class had arrived.

The Jeep's engine died, and its doors swung open. Like the other men in the lot, the one who jumped down from the passenger side was in excellent shape. He was probably six-two or so, and his T-shirt did nothing to hide the cords of muscle on his wide shoulders. But, it wasn't the passenger that snagged her attention.

The driver slammed his door and strode to the back liftgate. She didn't see his face, only the back of him, but his gait was familiar, with more swagger than his passenger. He was as tall as the other man, and just as broad-shouldered and slim-hipped. The tilt of his head as he tossed a few bags onto the ground, the set of his shoulders as he closed the back of the Jeep, though...if returning to the Redmond base was a blast from the past, this man was a punch to the gut.

"Lance."

She didn't realize she said his name out loud until Joe grunted. "Yes. Lance Roberts."

Meg hadn't needed his confirmation. She'd know Lance anywhere. After ten years, her body hadn't forgotten watching him, wishing he was hers, with the added misfortune of embodying the "little sister in love with brother's best friend" cliché.

Hard to forget embarrassment like that.

Lance the boy had been the stuff of her girlhood dreams, and more than a few other girls' dreams, too. As she watched, he grabbed his bags off the ground and the muscles of his forearms tightened. Heat stretched up her spine, warming her stomach.

Lance the man probably occupied more than a few women's dreams now as well.

Meg spun sideways, not wanting to be caught staring at him. "What's he doing here?" she whispered. She smoothed the end of her ponytail, and then tugged at her blouse, straightening imaginary wrinkles.

Catching herself, she squeezed her fingers together in front of her, forcing them still.

"Now, Meggy. I need you to be open-minded. And, I need your help with your brothers..." Joe's head dropped, and he rubbed the back of his head.

"Joe, what have you done?" There were only so many reasons that Lance would be here, at the air center, right now...

"I offered Lance a job, if he makes it through training." His half grin looked pained. "He'll be in this year's rookie training class."

* * * *

"Subtle, man." Dak Parrish, his helitack buddy from north California and fellow member of this year's Redmond rookie class, joined Lance behind his Jeep and slung one of the duffel bags over his shoulder. "That entrance planned or does this shit just come naturally to you?"

"Nowhere to hide, anyway," Lance answered under his breath. Besides, he didn't shy away from anything. "And I warned you. You could have come alone." He and Dak were coworkers, but arriving together revealed them as friends, too. Dak might regret that once he saw how things were here.

Dak's brows dropped, and he growled, "Don't insult me."

His friend's outrage made Lance smile, even though there wasn't much funny. For all his offers to do this alone, he was glad that Dak hadn't let him. He'd thought he was prepared to be back here, but apparently, he'd been wrong.

They unloaded the rest of their gear. He used the time to cast stealthy glances at the rest of the parking lot, trying to get his bearings.

When he and his mother moved away ten years ago, he hadn't expected to darken Redmond's community doorstep again. Being back at the air center, like this? Hadn't been on his radar.

He refused to squander this chance. He didn't give a shit if Redmond would rather see the back of him. He was going to prove that he belonged here, whether they liked it or not.

And once he did, he was going to find out the real circumstances around his father's death.

"Do all these people know you?" Dak had an uncanny knack for speaking without moving his lips.

"No. Not all of them. Some of them, probably." Lance ducked his head, shrugging his arms into his backpack. "Or they'll figure out who I am fast enough." He glanced at his friend. "I look exactly like my dad."

"Your dad," Dak repeated, his brow raised. "And that's a bad thing?"

Lance had told Dak that his father had died on the job—smokejumping—ten years ago. He'd left out that a lot of people in and around Redmond believed that his father's carelessness or recklessness, or both, had caused his death...and the death of his jump partner and best friend, Jason Buchanan.

"I guess we'll see." Lance clasped his friend on the shoulder, forcing his confident smile. He'd learned long ago how to hide behind it. "Let me show you around."

Weighed down by all their stuff, they trudged to the door. Only then did he catch sight of the redhead, standing at the entrance, talking with Joe Buchanan. She wasn't facing him, angled to the side, but he'd recognize her anywhere. He tensed, bracing for impact.

Dak whistled low. "Wow. Classy."

It took less than a second for him to figure out Dak was talking about the redhead and even less time than that for Lance's mood to darken. "Hands off."

The low, gravelly timber of his voice was nearly unrecognizable. But he definitely remembered the protective urge, the pull to this woman.

No, not this woman. The girl she'd been all those years ago. Hunter's kid sister.

Meg.

"It's like that, is it?" Dak chuckled.

"It's not like anything," Lance gritted out, dropping his gaze to his feet, unable to stare directly at her. It was like looking at the sun. "That's Meg Buchanan. She was my best friend's sister."

"Was your best friend's sister? She's not his sister anymore?" Dak was having fun with this.

"No, man." He shrugged, doing his best to hide the pang in his gut. "He's not my friend anymore."

That wiped the smile off Dak's face.

"Lance." The man beside Meg stepped toward him, his hand outstretched.

Joe Buchanan. He'd become the base manager shortly after Lance's father died. Joe sent him the official job offer last month.

When Lance learned they wanted to hire at least four new jumpers at Redmond, he hadn't hesitated to apply. That didn't mean he expected to be offered the job.

Considering whom his dad was, he expected them to laugh.

When he got the acceptance letter, he called. He didn't want to drive to Oregon for nothing. Joe assured him there was no mistake. Lance hadn't stayed on the line long. He thanked him, assured him that he'd be there, and disconnected.

Didn't want to give him an opportunity to renege. A chance like this, to get to the bottom of what happened with his father? He wouldn't pass it up.

Last year ago, he'd worked with a hotshot who'd been at Redmond when his father had been here. The guy probably wouldn't have said anything to him, now that Lance thought back on it, not if they hadn't saved each other's asses more than once. Because how his dad was blamed for someone's death? That shit didn't come up in everyday conversation.

But one night, over beers, the guy got all loose-lipped, going on about how what had happened to his father had been a damn shame, how it had been unfair that JT Roberts had been blamed so thoroughly for Jason Buchanan's death.

Lance hadn't said much. Didn't seem like good beer-drinking chatter. But, when he got home, he called his mom. She'd forwarded what the Forest Services' investigator had given her, and Lance had read that file dozens of times.

He had to admit he agreed with the guy.

So Redmond smokejumper training killed two birds with one stone. He'd dreamed of becoming a smokejumper forever. Like his father. Now he could do it here. Where his father had jumped.

And, maybe being at Redmond would help him flesh out what had really happened in that fire.

Now, he wondered if maybe this all was a cruel joke or some nasty karma he was working off. He hadn't expected to see Meg. He knew Will, her older brother, jumped at Redmond. But what was she doing here?

He shook Joe's hand. "Mr. Buchanan. Good to see you." He turned to Dak. "This is Dak Parrish. We rappelled together in California."

"Mr. Parrish. Nice to meet you." Joe's smile appeared genuine. He shook Dak's hand. "Welcome to Redmond Air Center, boys." He turned, then, to his niece. "Lance, you remember my niece, Meg, don't you?"

When she faced him, his first thought was that her adolescent pretty face had delivered on its promise. Meg, with her red hair and crystal blue eyes, had never been able to fade into the background, even then, even when she wanted to. The woman she'd grown into was striking. Pale skin, but not a hint of a freckle, as if they wouldn't dare. Her hair wasn't strawberry blonde, but auburn. And, those eyes…still the same sharp, smart eyes.

"Hey, firecracker."

The nickname rolled off his tongue, like it always had. He and Hunter used to call her that because she always held herself in check, but when she got angry, she was a sight to behold.

She'd hated it.

It was a mistake, too, to call her that here, in front of everyone. It was a bold-faced reminder of how close they had all been a lifetime ago. But he refused to pretend things were different. They had been close…once. And now they weren't. But, when her eyes lit, he didn't regret using the nickname one bit. He'd forgotten how much fun it was to ruffle Meg's feathers.

"Don't call me that." Where she'd been pale a moment ago, there was color in her cheeks, the prettiest pink. "We're not kids anymore, Lance."

"No. We're definitely all grown up." He let his gaze drift over her. Meg had always been tall, shooting up inches at a time in crazy growth spurts. But the girl he remembered had been thin, like a rubber band stretched too tight. The woman in front of him had grown into those long, lean limbs. Her legs went on for miles. She had a slim waist, and the arms she crossed over her pretty, high breasts were toned.

When his gaze returned to her face, his smile widened. Yep...the eyes were definitely still the same. The package might be different, but the fire was still there, and he still enjoyed riling her up.

"You look good, Meg." It was an understatement. She looked amazing. She glared at him, and then rolled her eyes.

"Guess they'll let anyone in here."

At the voice behind him, he closed his eyes, inhaling. Bracing himself. Another blast from the past. "Will."

He turned to find Meg's oldest brother, Will Buchanan, dropping his bag into the dirt and crossing his arms over his chest, a mirror of his sister's stance. Behind him, Hunter, his former best friend, stared at the far off mountains, his jaw tight. Both brothers looked the same, only older. Both were taller than average, like their sister, and the years had filled them out as well.

Well, he'd come a long way in the past decade, too. He'd hoped the time might have been long enough to let cooler heads prevail.

Apparently not.

"Joe," Will addressed his uncle. "Why is this piece of trash on our doorstep?"

Joe exhaled sharply, propping his fists on his hips. "Come on, now..."

Lance lifted his hand. "It's okay, Joe." He smiled. Maybe Will thought he could intimidate him. If so, the guy's memory must have failed since Lance moved away. "Good to see you, too, Will." He nodded his head toward Hunter. "Hunt. How are you?"

Hunter grunted, his expression guarded.

Though Will's glare never left him, his words were for Joe. "What the hell is he doing here?"

It seemed obvious, but maybe Will needed things spelled out. "I'm in the new rookie class."

"No way."

The way he said it, full of outrage, pissed Lance off. He stepped closer, meeting Will's eyes and getting right in his face. "I can assure you it's true. I have the paperwork to prove it."

Will didn't back down, and Lance hadn't expected him to. He'd spent years as a pseudo-brother to the guy. They had nearly matching hardheadedness.

As they stared at each other, any hopes that his return to Redmond wouldn't be a disaster died. It disappointed him to discover they'd existed at all.

Hope was for idealists. He was a survivor.

One thing was painfully clear: Will was going to make this hard for him. Maybe even impossible.

Well, he wasn't the sort to give up. If he wasn't going to make it through training, then he planned to go down swinging.

Meg stepped into the tension between them. Placing one hand on Will's chest, she rested the other over Lance's heart. He didn't look away from Will's gaze, but the heat from her palm seeped through his T-shirt. As it laced through him, it touched places inside he refused to examine.

"Stop it, Will," she whispered, looking up into her brother's face. "You're making a scene."

No one moved, not Will, not Meg, not him.

After another pregnant moment, she added, "Please. For me."

Will blew out, breaking the eye contact. With a fluid movement, he grabbed his bag from where he'd dropped it at his feet. He didn't say anything else as he swept inside the air center. Hunter followed, brushing past Lance without a word.

Meg retreated a few steps, and he missed her closeness. Her head dropped, and he remembered so many times when she'd played the peacemaker. He reached for her—maybe to touch her hand, he didn't know—but she stepped back and away. With an unreadable glance, she followed her brothers inside, leaving him staring after them all.

"So, that went well," Dak offered under his breath.

Lance snorted. But the exchange broke the spell. He turned to Joe who rubbed the back of his neck.

"Let's get you settled, then." The base manager's face had been welcoming earlier, but now it was lined with stress, making him appear much older. He moved to the door, holding it open for them as they gathered their stuff. "I put you on the far end, Lance…"

"Not my father's cubicle?" Will had taken his father's space, after he'd died. Lance had seen it, the one time he'd returned to the air center after the Blue Creek fire, to collect his dad's personal effects. His mom hadn't been able to stomach seeing the place.

"I figured you might not...what I mean is it might be best..."

Lance could see exactly what he meant. This was a chance to distance himself from his father's history. But Lance refused to delude himself. There was nowhere to run. "That's okay, Mr. Buchanan. I'll take my dad's space. Thanks."

As Joe nodded and ducked inside, Dak caught his sleeve. "What the hell happened here?" He nudged his chin toward the building. "Those people hate you."

This was not a conversation for the parking lot. "Let's get settled. Maybe we can get a beer later. I might need it."

Chapter 2

"It's been a decade, Will." Joe leaned back in his chair and folded his hands in front of him, probably attempting some calm in this mess. "It's time to let this go."

Will slammed his palm on the desk. Definitely not calm. "There's no statute of limitations on stuff like this."

Yeah, and the same could be said of Meg's attraction to Lance Roberts. Stupid girlhood crushes were supposed to end after one stopped being a stupid girl.

Apparently not.

Her palm still tingled from where she'd touched him. It had barely been any contact and through a shirt, for Christ's sake, yet it had hit her in the belly. She'd been holding her breath, worried what Will might do. But, if she was totally honest, it was hard to breathe close to Lance.

Stupid, stupid...

"He's earned the spot." Joe rubbed the back of his head. "Spent three years as a volunteer, then three on a hotshot crew. Since then, he's been on a helitack team in north California. If he passes the physical test tomorrow, and I have no reason to believe he won't, he can start the training."

"He shouldn't be on the team." Will had broken out his stubborn voice. He was the oldest, and for the past decade he'd been the patriarch of their dysfunctional family. Authoritative came easy.

She stifled her sigh. They didn't need outrage; they needed diplomacy. "I think you should let Joe do his job." Her brother swiveled to her, betrayal on his face. She lifted her hands in the universal sign of truce. "Think. He'd need referrals, recommendations. He probably went through at least a couple interviews. There are only four spots, so Joe probably offered chances to what, seven or eight people?" Pausing, she waited for Joe to nod in agreement. "You should entertain the thought that someone else might be a better judge of all things Lance Roberts than us."

Talk about putting things mildly. Between Will's irrational anger at finding him here, and her ridiculous attraction to him, they were definitely not unbiased bystanders. She should take her own advice.

"No, we're better judges than anyone. Those people don't have the one-on-one experience with him that we have. They don't know him."

"And what do you know about him? What do any of us really know now?" Will wasn't the only Buchanan with a temper, and her brother's over-the-top reaction was grating on her nerves. "That he used to be Hunter's best friend? That he spent more time at our house all those years ago than his own? That he was almost as much of a big brother to the twins as you guys are?" She snorted. "Or that he had the misfortune of being the son of a man who's been accused of being responsible for two needless deaths?"

Will's head jerked back. They never talked about their father's death. Today, though, it was too much of an elephant in the room.

She sighed. "It's been ten years since the fire, and almost that long since he and his mom moved away. A lot happens in that much time. Maybe we should give him a chance to prove us wrong. To prove everyone wrong." Shrugging, she wrapped her arms around her middle. "Things change. People change."

As if determined to prove her wrong, she caught sight of Lance out the window next to the door to Joe's office. He was emptying his bags into the locker that used to belong to his father. As he reached up, the muscles of his arms stretched the fabric of his T-shirt, showing off the equally cut expanse of his stomach. Turning, his broad shoulder and strong back filled her view, sending heat slicing into her stomach and hitching her breath.

When she looked at him, she didn't think about the Blue Creek fire or how his father was blamed for upending her family. Instead, she watched him move. He'd been handsome as a boy, with the smooth good looks of adolescence, but the man he'd become was more rugged, more chiseled. Harder, with more raw edges.

Just as sexy. More so, actually.

Sure, some things changed. But some things—like her reaction to him—didn't.

"You know what he was like, Meg." Will swung his arm out, encompassing Lance in the other room. "Reckless, a troublemaker. Always pushing the limits. Who talked you and Hunter into jumping the cliffs at the lake? Him. Skateboarding the rails when Hunter broke his arm? That was him, too. Skiing, racing ATVs, snowboarding…he took chances, drove too fast, and went too hard."

"You're one to talk. Yeah, he was an adrenaline junkie. And so were you." She smirked, and nudged her head toward Hunter. "And Hunter? He isn't? All of you guys are. You want to jump out of planes, into the middle of the wilderness, to fight fires. Don't preach at me how he's more dangerous than the rest of you." She stopped there. It was no secret to her brothers how she felt about what they did or how much it scared her.

If it was up to her, she'd never lose another loved one in a fire. That was one of many reasons why she wanted this job. She couldn't control the fires, but, as their trainer, she could control how prepared they were for them.

"It's different." Will rolled his eyes, his mouth thinning. "His father was like that, too. Always the first in, always the one to go hardest. Reckless. He convinced Dad to take stupid risks that day, the kind that got them stranded on the wrong side of the flame. And we know what happened after that."

The words hung in the air along with all the tension between them.

"He deserves a chance, Will," she whispered. Thinking that she'd gotten her job because of her last name, while Will wanted to keep Lance from his because of his father…it didn't sit well with her. "Everyone deserves a chance."

"I agree." Hunter shoved away from the wall where he'd been leaning, quiet until now. "Let it go, Will."

Will turned his glare on him for a long moment before pushing away from the desk. Standing, he flexed his fingers, studying them all. Finally, he nodded. "Fine. I'm outnumbered. But, I swear, Joe, I'm watching him. If he," he pointed at the door, "so much as steps one toe out of line, or puts anyone in danger, I'll make sure he's out of here. Even if it means going over your head."

Before any of them could respond, he stormed out. Meg exhaled a breath she hadn't been aware she'd been holding.

Grimly, Joe nodded to her and Hunter. "You two might as well get settled. It's going to be an interesting year."

She snorted, smiling in spite of herself. Talk about an understatement.

Her grin disappeared as she caught Hunter's expression. Her heart twisted. She'd been so caught up with how she was dealing with Lance's return that she hadn't considered how Hunter must be feeling. He and Lance had been as thick as thieves as kids, pretty much from the time they could crawl.

After the allegations about his father and the fire began to circulate, Lance stopped coming around. Meg had understood. He was grieving his own loss, and probably thought that her family hated him, too, if the rumors were true. Through it all, though, Hunter refused to give up on him. He'd called, left messages, invited him to get together. Not once or twice, but dozens of times.

By the time Lance and his mom left town, four months after the fire, they still hadn't spoken.

She squeezed his arm as she walked by. Under her breath, she said so only he could hear, "Just because he deserves a chance here doesn't mean he deserves a chance with us."

She purposely added herself into the mix. If anyone needed a reminder that Lance wouldn't be good for them, that he wasn't a risk worth taking, it was her.

Not only because he'd never given her the time of the day, no matter how many times she'd thrown herself at him. Looking back, it had been painfully obvious how she'd felt about him. Teenage girls weren't usually subtle, and she'd been no exception.

No, it wasn't only that, though that should do it.

She was going to be the assistant trainer here, at rookie training, for the next four weeks. She'd wanted this job for a long time and she wouldn't jeopardize it.

At the end, he would be a smokejumper, the most elite kind of firefighter. The job that had killed her father. She would never allow herself to get involved with one of them.

Which meant she needed to squash this stupid attraction. Because people with stupid crushes did stupid things. So, she would be her professional best with Lance Roberts. The rest of the time, she'd stay far away from him.

* * * *

"Hear you made quite the entrance at the air center." Lance's grandmother didn't look up from her knitting. Her conversation starters were like guerrilla warfare: no warning, surprise attacks.

Grinning, he dropped the food he'd picked up on the counter. There were groceries, but only staples, because he wasn't sure what she needed. He hadn't called, though, because if he'd asked what she needed, she would have chewed him out about how she could take care of herself. He'd picked up dinner, anyway. Takeout would have to do because he wasn't much of a cook. The restaurant scene hadn't changed much in Redmond over the years. Lots of Mexican and pizza joints. He'd grabbed some sandwiches and salads. And, of course, some coffee.

Gram was like him. She had no internal clock that decided it was too late for coffee. For them, coffee was an all-day affair.

He sauntered over, kissed her papery cheek, and set the to-go cup next to her. As she glanced up at him over her bifocals, he did his best not to squirm under her astute gaze. Gram was still sharp as a whip at eighty-three. Staring him down, she retrieved her cup.

After a drink, she nodded and set it down. Testing his order accuracy. It was exactly the way she liked it, heavy on the cream, no sugar. Because he remembered stuff like that.

"Wasn't going to slink in, Gram." He sipped from his own cup. "I haven't done anything wrong." Even now, hours later, his temper flared. Will and Hunter...they'd treated him like a criminal.

Whatever. Not his problem. Sure, they could make things harder for him, spread rumors, but nothing they did would affect whether he passed through training or not.

He wasn't going anywhere.

She harrumphed, returning to her needles. He chuckled and returned to the kitchen to unload the rest of the groceries he'd brought her.

He didn't get here to visit as often as he liked, only a few times a year. Since he and his mom moved to California, after his father died, his mom had no desire to return. This had been her husband's hometown, after all, and she and Gram had never gotten along. She'd only moved here because this was where he'd wanted to jump. With him gone, she'd moved south. It was warmer there, she said.

Lance thought she just couldn't take the whispers any more.

"Heard the Buchanan girl's going to be one of the assistant trainers." Gram's words ripped through the silence and stilled his hands.

Was she talking about Meg? "What?"

She glanced at him again, her brows lifted over her glasses. "There's only one Buchanan girl, isn't there?"

"Yes. That part, yes." He waved his hand. "The other, though. What do you mean assistant trainer?" Surely the world couldn't be this cruel.

"Heard it from Harriet. Her grandson's on the hotshot crew. He's friends with Bobby Mitchell, the head physical trainer at the air center." She pointed a crooked finger at him. "Said that the Buchanan girl would be Bobby's assistant this year."

He propped himself on his hands, letting his head fall between his shoulders and closed his eyes.

Damn it. He hadn't asked why Meg was at the air center. He usually had such attention to detail. She wasn't a firefighter. Gran had told him in passing, during another trip, that she'd gone to school to be a physician's assistant, at University of Washington. She shouldn't have any reason to be at the air center.

For him, though, the Buchanans were a package deal. He'd grown up with the three of them, and he bet that if the twins had been older, he would have hung out with them, too. They'd all been a family. So having her there, with her brothers, had seemed normal.

"Assistant trainer, huh?" Of course. Because the universe hated him.

"That's what I hear. She's always running those marathons and whatnot. Can't even go to church without hearing some other damn thing that girl has excelled at." Gram snorted.

Lance opened his mouth to defend her, but stopped when she looked at him expectantly. He snapped his lips closed. Anything he said would give too much away.

He turned, to shield his face from his shrewd grandmother. He hated to admit how much he kept tabs on the Buchanans, especially Hunter and, to an uncomfortable extent, Meg. Hunter was to be expected. They'd been friends forever, and he hated how he'd left things between them. He missed the guy. Before their meeting today, he'd thought he might be able to explain things. Mend fences.

Now, he doubted it. With them vying for the same jobs, and thanks to the past, he didn't think there'd be room to patch things up.

His interest in Meg was more complicated.

As his best friend's kid sister, she'd been off limits his entire life. He'd tried to pretend she was his sister, too. He didn't have any siblings, and when he was around the Buchanans, he desperately wanted some.

Then high school began, and it became harder to pretend his feelings were sisterly. There was something between them, something awake and aware. When they were alone, he couldn't ignore the weight in the spaces between their bodies. Sometimes, she studied him expectantly. As if she sensed it, too.

Except she was Hunter's sister. Hands off.

So they'd been friends, and he'd buried the rest of his wishful thinking, right where the sun didn't shine.

It stayed there, too, except that one time, the spring before their fathers died. She'd been upset about something, he couldn't remember what. He'd hugged her on her parents' porch, and somehow, she'd ended looking up at him, her blue eyes full of unshed tears. He'd run his thumb over her cheekbone, desire raging through his nearly seventeen-year-old body, hot and needy.

Tilting her head back, she closed her eyes and leaned into him.

It had taken everything he had to step backward, to grip her shoulders and set her away from him, when everything inside him screamed to pull her close, to cover her soft mouth with his.

Her eyes had flared open, and a flush had lit her features like a torch. She'd muttered something unintelligible before running inside. Letting her go had twisted his stomach.

After that, things were different. She'd been stiffer with him, artificial. Probably not apparent to anyone else, but he'd known. In his desperation to change nothing between them all, he'd ruined everything.

Their fathers died, then, and he was gone.

Today, he drank her in, like a man who'd crossed a desert and was dying of thirst. He'd realized, seeing her again, that she was as inaccessible now as she'd been all those years ago. Not because of his loyalty to her brothers, her family, but because she and her family wanted nothing to do with him now.

It had bothered him, and he'd lost his temper. That had been stupid. If he'd kept his cool, he would have handled Will better...especially if he'd known Meg was going to be his physical trainer.

If he planned to prove that he'd outgrown his adolescent hotheadedness, he was off to a bad start.

Tomorrow, he needed to pass his physical test. He didn't expect any problems. He was in the best shape of his life. But he couldn't afford unnecessary enemies, especially when they had the power to get him thrown out of the program.

Perfect. Leave it to him to get off on the wrong foot before he even started the damn training.

He could fix this. Tomorrow, he would apologize for stirring things up with Will. She shouldn't have had to interfere in that situation. Then he needed to back way off from her. The less direct contact, the better. Head down, get through this training. That was his new mantra.

Meg Buchanan had always been a soft spot for him. He couldn't afford that now.

If he was going to find out what happened with his dad in that fire, he needed to be here, in Redmond, to do it. There was no better place to fill in the holes in the official story. That meant he needed to be a smokejumper here, whatever it took.

He rubbed his hand over his face. Meg had stepped between him and Will, had defused what could have been an uglier scene. She'd always been the peacemaker, the one with the rod of steel in her spine who'd kept the testosterone of her siblings in check, never letting them go too far.

On some level, she still saw him as someone worth going to bat for. That had to mean something.

Maybe if he could talk to her, explain, say he was sorry…it was worth a shot.

"Does Meg still live in Bend?" he asked Gram. She'd know. She knew everything.

"Yes." She didn't pause in her stitches. "But, she's probably at her mother's."

"Yeah?" He swiped his keys off the counter, and shoved them in his jeans pocket.

Gram reached for her scissors, not looking at him. "Always goes there when she's in town. Good thing, too. Woman's house is a mess. Needs all the help she can get."

"Thanks," he interrupted, before Gram could launch into a longer diatribe against Meg's mother. He didn't know where Gram got her intel, but he never doubted it. He swept forward, dropping another kiss on her cheek. "I'll be back in a little bit."

"Did you bring me food?" She called after him. "I'm starving."

Smiling, he paused in the kitchen to put half a sandwich and some pasta salad on a paper plate for her. Then, he set the food up on a tray table beside her. She patted his cheek, briefly holding his eyes. "You're a good boy." She sniffed. "Even if you don't come and visit your grandmother enough."

He laughed. "Don't clean that up. I'll put it away for you when I get back." Gram still got around well, but he worried when she moved things.

"Don't tell me what to do in my own home, child."

He chuckled again, locking the door behind him.

Chapter 3

As always, Meg's mom's house was a disaster.

Meg started cleaning, per her usual, in the kitchen. Dishes and counters. She dragged Ethan away from the Xbox and he was sweeping. Kyle hadn't surfaced yet, but when he did, he could man the vacuum.

Opening the trash receptacle made her gag. "When is the last time anyone cleaned this out?"

Ethan shrugged, still unhappy that she'd interrupted his "Call of Duty" game.

Covering her mouth, she hightailed it out the backdoor, dumping the contents of the thing into the outdoor garbage can. Snagging the hose, she filled the bin with water and left it there to soak.

Stomping inside, she opened the cabinet under the sink. Sure enough, there was an unopened bag of trash bags. No one had bothered to put one in the can, so the inside of the thing was a science experiment. "Ethan. You guys need to put trash bags in the garbage can. It's nasty."

Her brother lifted his shoulders again. "Mom doesn't care."

Their mother didn't care about much of anything. "Not the point. It should have the liner. Do it for me. It's disgusting."

He rolled his eyes. At fourteen, the eye rolls were strong with this one.

The sound of tires on the driveway drew her attention. Her mother's older model Ford Explorer ground to a halt outside the window.

Meg had hoped to make more progress before she got home. The dishes were still soaking.

Her mom came in, still in her nursing scrubs. "Why's the trash can outside?"

"Because it was nasty." Meg waved a hand over the kitchen, taking in the sticky counters and dirty floors. "This is pretty gross, too."

Ethan propped the broom on the wall, patting his hands on his legs. "I'm out of here." With that, her brother beat a hasty retreat as if he could smell the upcoming argument.

That wasn't the issue, though. It was fine if he didn't want to be around for the fight. What bothered her was that her mother let him go. It looked like she let Ethan and Kyle get away with a lot these days.

Karen Buchanan sighed, dropping her handbag on the kitchen table, on top of whatever was already sitting there. She wore weariness like a secondhand coat that didn't quite fit. Meg didn't remember her mother being this tired when she was a child, but since her father's death, exhaustion seemed like all she could manage. "I know. I've meant to clean this week, but it got away from me."

This week? It looked like the kitchen hadn't seen cleaning supplies since Meg had been here three weeks ago. She didn't think that would be a helpful observation, though.

"Why aren't you making the twins help out around here?" She pointed after Ethan. "Like that. You'd have never let Will, Hunter, or me get away with that."

"Meg, it's hard, being a single mom…"

She'd heard some incarnation of this speech more than a few times over the past couple of years. Lifting her hand, she stopped the excuses. "I hear."

Her mother's face fell.

Sighing, she placed her hands on her hips. This wasn't fair. Her mother hadn't invited her to come here and ambush her when she got home from work. The place was always a disaster when Meg got here. This was nothing new. She was taking her shitty day, seeing Lance again, all of it, out on her.

Her mother watched her warily, her dark hair pulled in a low ponytail, not much different than the one Meg wore today. But, it was disheveled, with lots of wayward wisps. Without a stitch of makeup, her mom looked at least ten years older than her true age.

Stepping forward, Meg folded the woman who used to bake her cookies into a hug. They stood like that for a long minute. Closing her eyes, Meg breathed in her mother's familiar smell. Finally, she pulled away and smoothed her mom's hair back, behind her ears. "Go get showered. I'm making lasagna."

Her mother's eyes looked shiny, but she nodded, swallowing hard. Snagging her bag, she left Meg alone in the kitchen.

She leaned against the sink, staring out the window.

Since Meg had moved to Bend, her mother seemed even worse than she used to be. If she was one of Meg's patients, Meg would suggest antidepressants. She'd even mentioned them in passing on a few occasions over the years, but her mother had only gotten angry. Then she'd improve for a few months only to sink back into herself again.

Why did everything here, in Redmond, feel unbalanced? In Bend, she lived an orderly life, in her tidy one-bedroom apartment. She had a few good friends she had drinks with after work, had begun dating one of the doctors at the hospital there, Shawn. It was casual, and even after a few months, it hadn't gotten any more serious. But she liked him. He was like her: enjoyed good food, good wine, and quiet conversation.

It was normal. Maybe even a little boring.

But when she got home, in this town, everything became so complicated.

As if to punctuate how problematic things were, the open window admitted the sound of a loud muffler outside. She'd already heard that noise once today.

Pushing away from the sink, she stepped out on the back porch as Lance's Jeep came into view down her mom's winding driveway. As he parked behind her mom's Explorer and killed the engine, she glanced behind her, hoping that her brothers—and definitely her mother—didn't come investigate. She'd already had her fill of family drama for the day.

The sound of her mom's shower running filtered through the wall. Ethan was probably buried in his headphones and COD. Safe.

The driver's door swung wide, and Lance jumped down. Pulling his mirrored aviators off his face, he tossed them onto the seat before slamming the door behind him.

Damn it, why did he have to look so good? He tucked his hands into his jeans pockets, and the stance accentuated the cut muscles of his arms and chest. Glancing up at her on the porch, he squinted into the late afternoon sunshine, leveling her with his signature confident grin. "Hey."

"What are you doing here?" All the frustration of the day swirled through her, making her voice testier than she would have liked. "My mom just got home." She didn't add that she doubted her mother would want to see him, but it hung unsaid, in the air.

His grin faltered slightly before slipping back in place. Like it was some mask he wore. "How's Mrs. B?"

That's what he used to call her, all through their childhood. The way he said it made her heart clench. "She's fine." It was a lie, but she wasn't talking about it with him. "Why are you here?" she asked again.

"Listen, Meg…" He tilted his head. "Can you come down? Sit with me? I only need a minute." He lifted his hands in an 'I'm innocent' gesture. "I'm harmless. Swear. For old times' sake."

She should send him away. Starting tomorrow, she was going to be his trainer and this conversation probably wasn't professional. But, she'd watched his face while Will ragged on him. He'd looked pained.

The memory of that look guided her off the porch. She sat on the second to last step.

His grin this time was more like the smiles she remembered, wide and genuine. Her stomach flipped, and girlish butterflies danced in there. She ignored them.

He lowered himself beside her. "I wanted to apologize."

That had been the last thing she expected him to say. The Lance she used to know didn't say he was sorry. "Apologize?"

"Yes. I behaved badly, at the air center." He swiped his hands over his hair. There were already peaks and valleys in it, as if he'd been running his fingers through it all day. "I shouldn't have let Will get to me."

She shrugged. "No problem."

He rubbed the back of his neck. "Yeah, it was. I was stupid." He glanced at her. "You shouldn't have had to step in. I put you in a bad position."

Thinking about standing next to him and touching him sent heat creeping up her neck. She resisted the urge to duck her head. Stupid pale skin.

Despite her flushed face, she hated watching *his* discomfort. She propped her elbows on her knees and nudged her shoulder against his. "It's over. I can handle it. Like you said, I'm all grown up."

She meant it to sound teasing. That would have been bad enough, falling back into bad habits, joking around with him like old times. Something about being here, on her mom's porch, the site of more than a few late-night conversations with Lance, had her twisted up.

But when his gaze met hers, his eyes were hot. As they raked her face, her stomach warmed, and tingles shimmered from there to her toes. She clasped her hands together so tightly that she was afraid she might break something.

He glanced into the woods next to her mother's property, and when he looked back, the heat was gone. As if she'd imagined it. He chuckled. "That you are."

Shrugging, she scrambled to recover her wits, to pretend she wasn't affected at all, while simultaneously wishing her blush would disappear.

"You're going to be the assistant physical trainer." His words, spoken at the trees in front of them, made all the butterflies in her belly die.

She laughed, standing, needing some distance. Of course. Why else would he come looking for her? He was worried that she'd ruin his chances at training. While she sat there hyperaware of him, he'd been watching his back.

As she paced away from him, she tried to regulate her breathing, like she did when she wanted to lower her heart rate on a run. "That's right. I'll be in charge of the actual physical training. Bobby Mitchell is going to retain control of the testing and the safety training. There are other trainers for the coursework." She had met them today. They all seemed nice enough. She hoped they'd make a cohesive team. "Mitch had some back issues last year. He isn't able to do the runs and pack-outs like he used to."

Lance nodded. "I'm not leaving training." His eyes burned up at her, but this time she recognized the fire. This was the ambition she remembered. All his life, Lance would decide he wanted something and then pursue it with single-minded focus. If he wanted to be here, to be a smokejumper, he was going to do whatever it took to make sure that happened. Even visit her at her mom's house and try to make nice.

"I know." She hugged her arms around her. "That's what I told Will today."

"Really?" His brows shot up.

"Sure. For the most part." She shrugged one shoulder, and inhaled. "He thinks you're reckless and dangerous. An adrenaline junkie, like your dad."

"Like Will's got room to talk."

"That's what I told him." She couldn't help her grin. "I also said that you deserved a chance, to prove yourself."

"You did?" His surprise was audible.

"Of course." She scowled. "You know me. It might have been ten years, but I haven't changed that much."

As he held her gaze, the years fell away, dragging them back to when they used to be friends, when she wished they could have been so much more. "Thank you."

"Is that why you came? To see if I'd make you quit training?"

He rubbed the back of his neck. "Well, you and your brothers didn't exactly welcome me with open arms."

He had, then. Sure, Will had wanted exactly that. She'd understand if Lance had seen that coming. But her? Even if she hadn't made the kind of lasting impression she'd always wanted to make, he must know she wouldn't agree to that. Things might be different between all of them now, but still…that stung.

She gritted her teeth, but kept her response mild. "We were surprised. No one told us you were coming."

His mouth thinned. "So you won't try to get me to quit?"

"No, you ass. As far as I'm concerned, you're just another trainee." It really chafed that he thought she'd be unfair to him. "Just like everyone else."

How she managed to deliver that lie was beyond her.

"Am I, Meg?" He pressed up, off the porch step, and closed the distance between them. When only a few inches separated them, he stopped. The close proximity forced her to look up at him, exposing her neck. She didn't step back, though, refusing to retreat from him. She was going to be his trainer, after all. An authority figure. She couldn't back down now.

"You are," she said, but it came out as a whisper. "We aren't friends. Not anymore. Not now, after everything." He'd opened a huge chasm between their families after the fire. He'd avoided them all and moved without even saying goodbye.

"I suppose not." His breath fanned her face, and her foolish body shivered. His hands dropped to cup her shoulders. There was no pressure, only his fingers on her, but she found herself leaning. Into him.

She'd been staring at his forehead, but now she couldn't keep from meeting his eyes.

The intensity there sent a lightning bolt through her. As she stared at him, she bit into her lower lip and his gaze strayed there. She wondered what it would be like to step closer, to reach for him, to put her hands on his waist, dig her fingers into his T-shirt and pull him toward her.

She tilted, a fraction of a shift, as if he was her sun and she was caught in his orbit.

Then, he glanced away and stepped back.

Embarrassment crashed down on her, her facing warming. Good God, what had she been about to do? She'd been contemplating throwing herself at him, that's what.

Firming her shoulders, she wrapped her hands around her waist. She'd been through this with him before, hadn't she? He'd never wanted to hurt her feelings. Since he moved, and she'd gained some space from him, that's the conclusion she'd reached. He must have known how she felt, but he'd chosen not to act on it, so he didn't embarrass her.

Because he hadn't felt the same.

Now, though, thinking he was protecting her or sparing her feelings only made it more pathetic. How many years would it take until she stopped being so attracted to Lance Roberts?

More than ten, obviously.

She was going to be his trainer. She'd have some control over whether he was hired at the end of all this. Having any physical contact with a rookie smokejumper—any smokejumper—would be completely unprofessional and could jeopardize her job.

If all those years of Lance showing no interest hadn't kept her in check, the risk he posed to her career should.

No more. She couldn't do her job, not like this. From here on, she was determined not to feel anything for him.

Nothing.

She attempted to ignore how good the late-day sun looked on his tanned skin, how soft his gray eyes were. Failed. "I can understand your concerns, Lance, but trust me, you and I are strictly professionals." She glared at him. "In fact, I plan to pretend you don't exist."

Lifting his hands, he said, "That's seems a bit extreme, doesn't—"

"And, I don't date firefighters, especially the ones I train. From here on, you won't touch me. At all." To prove her resolve, she stepped back. Because she couldn't think when he was this close and definitely not when his hands were on him.

His jaw tightened. It might have been ten years, but she recognized that look. It was a challenge. "Seems presumptuous. I didn't ask you out."

She continued as if he hadn't spoken. "No pat on the back, no nudge on the shoulder." She sounded crazy. This was too far. Or maybe it wasn't. Who knew? "Nothing."

"I understood what you meant." He snorted. "You know what, firecracker, that sounds good to me. Strictly professional. And trust me, I won't touch you at all. Nothing." Then, he offered her a grin that heated her blood. "Not unless you ask me to, anyway."

The image of her asking him to touch her…of him touching her because she asked…it sent a shiver of desire tiptoeing through her stomach. To cover any trace of that, she laughed. "Then you'll be waiting forever."

"Maybe." He offered her a jaunty salute. "Thanks for clearing this all up. It was…illuminating." He chuckled. "I'll see you tomorrow, firecracker."

He didn't wait for her to answer, only got in the Jeep and left.

She'd gotten good at watching Lance Roberts leave.

* * * *

As Lance navigated the turn from the Buchanan's gravel driveway onto the highway and accelerated toward the air center, he tilted his neck to one side, then the other, trying to stretch out the strain it had taken to joke his way out of that conversation. His palms were slick on the steering wheel, and he rubbed them one at a time against his pant legs. Even some distance didn't help the hum inside him. God, Meg's lips had looked so soft, her skin so smooth....

What the hell had he been thinking?

He never should have touched her. It was a recipe for disaster. He'd known, and he'd done it anyway. It was dangerous. Considering that he jumped out of planes, dived off cliffs, skied, surfed, and bungee jumped... that was saying something.

He'd dropped his hands on her shoulders, and the slim bones under his palms had made him want to tug her against him, pull her closer, feel her heat against him. The whole thing had gone straight to his head, like the sweetest adrenaline rush.

He needed to find out what happened to his father. One day after his return to Redmond and already he could see the Buchanans weren't going to appreciate him poking around. Like the rest of the town, they believed his dad had left them fatherless. None of them seemed willing to rehash that history.

Well, he owed it to his father to see this through. Owed it to himself. He'd lost everything in that fire, too.

His father's memory had taken such a beating after his death. His grandmother had hardened, thanks to all the public scrutiny. Unable to take it, his mother had fled town with as much dignity as she could muster.

There were so many pieces missing from the events of that day. Only Joe Buchanan had been on the ground at the fire with Jason Buchanan and JT Roberts. Traumatized after his brother's death and suffering from PTSD, he hadn't been reliable, and his testimony had been disregarded for the most part. Now, years later, Lance hoped that Joe could piece some of it together for him. Maybe the pilot from that day, or one of the other jumpers could help, too. Someone had to know something.

As he planned his return, he'd known that if he discovered something that exonerated his father—even partially—it could defame the Buchanans. He'd told himself that it couldn't be helped. Any discomfort to the Buchanans would be the necessary result for unearthing the truth.

He only wanted the truth. After a decade, he needed it.

Seeing Will and Hunter today...he didn't care if he found something that pissed them off.

But Meg? He wouldn't hurt Meg intentionally for anything.

They couldn't be friends anymore, and they definitely couldn't be more. Even the truce he'd offered her would feel like a betrayal if he discovered something that ruined her memory of her father. Which is why he needed to avoid near misses like what happened on her porch, no matter the cost.

He meant what he'd said. He wouldn't touch her again. Even if it killed him.

Meg wasn't a rule breaker. There shouldn't be anything between them, not if they didn't want to complicate their jobs. She'd make sure they did the right thing.

He might not have it in him to do what was appropriate, but he trusted Meg.

Because if it was up to him, right thing be damned. God, he'd wanted to kiss her. He still ached with it. She'd been going on, about how he was like everyone else, and something in him had growled.

He'd always wanted to be someone important to her, more than just her brother's friend, but he'd never allowed himself to think of Meg like that. Or, when he had those stirrings, he squashed them. She was Hunter's sister. Guys didn't chase their best friend's kid sisters. It was unspoken bro code.

He and Hunter didn't talk anymore. Yesterday, he'd barely looked at him.

Maybe that's what kicked his libido into overdrive. Some unspoken barrier that had kept him from thinking of Meg like that had been removed. And the feel of her under his fingertips, the sound of her sigh as she stepped closer…it had cut straight to his groin. He'd wanted to cover her mouth, hold her close, kiss her again and again until they were breathless.

She'd told him she wouldn't ask him to touch her again. He should want her to keep that promise. He didn't.

He needed to knock this shit off. Nothing would ruin his chances here faster than hitting on his trainer. In the end, nothing would hurt her more than if he let his desire for her get the best of him while he kept secrets from her.

As he turned into the air center parking lot, he slowed over the gravel and pulled his Jeep into a spot in the back. Shifting into park, he rounded his shoulders and exhaled.

His fired-up sex drive might want one thing, but rationality needed to prevail. He'd learned what he needed to know from her: she wouldn't stand in his way during training. It might have been a decade, but Meg had always been true to her word.

He would leave it at that. Tomorrow, he would pass his test, the first step toward becoming a smokejumper. Then, he would discover what really happened to his father.

Chapter 4

Last night, the rookies had been briefed on what they could expect today. At six o'clock in the morning, as the dew still covered the grass on the field behind the air center, Meg stood in front of the new smokejumper recruits. She listened to a few of the seasoned smokejumpers as they explained the physical test and reinforced the seriousness of their training. They were an intimidating sight. If the rookies weren't quaking in their boots yet, they should be.

After the fire and brimstone speech, they headed for the community college where they'd do the PT test. None of them said much. She supposed that's what happened when a group of men waited for a life-changing milestone to be completed. If they didn't pass, they'd go home and take their dreams of smokejumping with them.

Her job might not be on the line, but she was wrestling with her own demons.

At four o'clock, unable to sleep, she'd scoured the coffee carafe, removing weeks of grime. Then, she drank an entire pot as she flipped through the files of all of the firefighters in front of her.

She read Lance's twice. His references praised his attention to detail and leadership skills. They admired his charisma and cautioned about his stubborn streak.

None of it surprised her. What she didn't expect—and had been completely inconvenient—was how proud she was of him. Beneath the weight of his father's scandal, he could have chosen a different path. She'd have understood if he had.

After all, she'd abandoned her own desire to take up firefighting when she couldn't handle what happened back then.

But, like her brothers, Lance had picked the career that their fathers loved, a calling they'd all admired as children. A job that caused her icy worry any time she thought too long about her brothers doing it.

From what she read, he'd become a damn good firefighter.

Which should have reinforced how unsuitable he was for her. If their history didn't make him off limits, the fact that he was a firefighter should put him squarely in the "hell no" category.

Her mother died slowly in the years after losing the love of her life to firefighting. She wouldn't repeat that mistake.

She dated safe men. In college, she'd chosen accountants and businessmen. Shawn, the guy she was casually dating now, was a doctor.

So what if Shawn and the others never made her stomach fluttery like Lance did? At least men like Shawn didn't risk their lives for a living.

Her misstep last night couldn't be repeated. If she was going to prove to Lance—to herself—that he was no different than the other recruits, she needed to start today.

Before she left her mom's house, she'd tied her hair into a ponytail. Then, she braided it. When the braid didn't look right, she pulled it out, chastised herself for being silly, and refastened the ponytail.

It didn't matter what she looked like. She would run these guys through their physical tests. Lance was just one of the recruits. Like all the others.

She needed to start believing that, or she would sabotage herself here before she had a chance to call this a career.

As they filed into the college gym, she followed, surveying the group.

They really were impressive. As they stood at attention, they looked like a bunch of calendar models: rugged, determined, and in amazing shape. Their files proved again that her uncle was an astute judge of what it took to be a superior firefighter.

While three of them—Hunter included—came from the Redmond hotshot crew, the other four were outsiders. All of Lance and Dak's experience was in California. The man they were calling Digger had been part of the Missoula hotshots. He didn't say much, but his referrals claimed he was the "keep your mouth shut and do the job" sort. She admired that. The determined tilt of his chin said he planned to be one of the last men standing.

The other guy, Rock, was trying out for the part of class clown. The sun was barely up and the guy was already cracking jokes.

As for the other guys from Redmond, Hunter hadn't told her much. Sledge and Kevin. Sledge—short for Sledgehammer, she was told—was the typical overachiever. Even this early, his hair was slicked, and he wore the expression of someone who expected and accepted only perfection. On the other hand, Kevin's skin was pale. Probably test day nerves. Well, if he couldn't guts it out through a physical, he wasn't going to hack it jumping from a plane into a fire. The sooner they all figured that out, the better.

The veteran jumpers explained the PT test, peppered with a heavy dose of "this isn't going to be easy" fear tactics, and they handed the group over to the trainers: today, her and her boss, Bobby Mitchell.

"Good morning." Mitch clasped his clipboard in front of him. "I'm the head trainer. This here is Meg Buchanan, one of my assistants. Pass this test, you stay. Fail, you're gone. We start with pull-ups, push-ups, and sit-ups. You manage that, we'll take a mile and a half run. Then, the pack test. You'll carry 110-pound packs and we'll walk a few miles. All before lunch. It's going to be a great morning."

He pointed to Lance, Dak, and Rock. "You three with Meg. I'll take the rest of you."

Nodding, she gripped her own clipboard and stopwatch. She'd been avoiding Lance's eyes, but now she couldn't. The connection sent a flurry of butterflies dancing in her stomach. God, he looked amazing…and determined. His shoulders were tight, his jaw firm. The weight of his gaze bored into her. She had to tear her eyes away.

Inhaling a steadying breath, she forced a smile and hoped it looked confident. She could do this. "We'll take turns. I'll time you for each task. Let's begin with pull-ups or chin-ups. For this, you need to get your jawbone over the bar."

She glanced at each of them, making sure to spend the same amount of time on each face, doing her best not to linger on Lance. "Who would like to go first?"

"I'll go." Lance stepped forward. "Lead the way."

She nudged her head toward the bar anchored on the wall. His eyes fixed on the bar above his head and he stripped out of the sweatshirt he'd been wearing, leaving himself in a thin, blue T-shirt. To distract herself from the set of his shoulders and the ripple of muscle beneath the fabric, she busied herself with the stopwatch. "You need to do seven. I'll time you."

He nodded, though he undoubtedly was well versed on the specifics of the test. With a leap, he gripped the bar, hanging. The muscles along his arms played and she bit into her lip. "Tell me when," he said.

"Go," she said, clicking the button on the watch.

Though there was a standardized time to complete the exercise, he easily beat it. In rapid succession, he lifted himself up, clearing the bar with his chin over and over. He made it look easy. Dropping to the ground when he was done, he folded his arms over his chest and smiled at her, his breathing barely labored. "Good?"

She nodded. More than good. They'd been perfect. And, he'd looked amazing doing them, damn it. Swallowing, she licked her top lip. "Yeah. Those were all fine."

Did she sound breathless?

He shrugged. "I know."

As he joined Dak, her brow furrowed, and her mouth thinned. "Charming."

He laughed. She glared at him, but stopped herself from saying more. He was right. They had been good.

"Dak, you're next," she deflected, because she was supposed to be in charge.

Lance's friend nodded. Without a word, he jumped up and clasped the bar. She clicked the stopwatch again. "Go."

Dak completed his set easily as well, though maybe not as fast or as smoothly as Lance. When he hopped down and rolled his shoulders, Rock folded his arms over his chest. "Jesus, you should have let me go first. Hard to look properly macho with these guys around."

Not that he should have worried. When she hit the stopwatch, he did fine. Maybe not as fast or as clean as Dak and Lance, but he still managed the minimum.

"Great," she said, marking down their times on her sheet. "Now, forty-five sit-ups and twenty-five push-ups."

She timed them. They all managed the task, though Rock struggled the most.

Again, though, Lance proved he was in better shape than either of the others. Except now, he was covered in a fine layer of sweat. She did her best to pretend that sweat didn't look better on him than it looked on the others. With the three tasks done, they rejoined Mitch and she gritted her teeth.

She was his trainer, and he was a rookie at training, a rookie she was supposed to judge without bias. She'd told herself she could do this, that she could ignore him and treat him like everyone else.

Maybe she was wrong.

In the van on the way to the run course, she forced herself to revisit everything that happened last night. As she'd lain in bed, she'd allowed her embarrassment to settle in her gut. No matter what she'd said to Lance, no matter how she'd tried to blame him, it wasn't his fault she was attracted to him. She'd been seconds from falling into him. She wanted him to kiss her, the same as she'd always wanted him to kiss her, all those years ago. She'd covered it in bravado, brushing him off afterward. Alone last night, in the bed where she'd dreamed of him as a girl, she couldn't pretend she didn't want him. Again. Still, maybe. When he'd touched her, the shiver along her spine had settled in her belly in ways she'd never experienced before.

She couldn't let that affect what she was doing here.

This was the first day of training, and she needed to judge Lance and his progress fairly. If she couldn't get a handle on this ridiculous attraction, she would need to recuse herself from her position. Not only would that be highly unprofessional, but how was she going to explain that to her brothers? To her mother and Uncle Joe? That she couldn't stop staring at Lance Roberts's butt and that was messing with her ability to do her job?

She'd never live it down. She'd never forgive herself.

She'd taken this job so she could ensure smokejumpers' safety. She needed to make sure that no other families went through what hers had. Though she'd never been able to master her fear of fire, the need to serve, to help others, it was as much a part of her and her family as their Irish temperaments. This job—training these highly specialized firefighters how to be as safe and prepared as possible—was her way of contributing.

It was bad enough she was putting that goal at risk, but even entertaining an attraction to a firefighter, let alone the most dangerous type of firefighting? What was she thinking? She'd watched her mother these past years, struggling with the loss of the man she loved. She refused to follow her path. It was hard enough knowing that her brothers risked their lives, that she might lose them to a flame someday. She might not be able to control her brothers' choices, but she could decide her own fate. She chose not to fall in love with a firefighter.

And without a doubt, Lance Roberts was a firefighter...and a man she could love. She'd been half in love with him her entire life. That's why she needed to stop this. Now.

A good run would help her shake this off. It usually did. When they reached the course, she called to Mitch, "I'll lead the pack on the run test." Unzipping her fleece, she dropped it next to the guys' water bottles and Gatorades. She pulled her arm across her chest, stretching her shoulder.

Rock laughed. "All respect, Ms. Buchanan, but I'll be leading the pack." He crossed his arms over his chest, smirking.

She smiled. She didn't have any faith in her choices in men right now, but she knew she was a good runner. From the looks of them, a lot of these guys ran frequently. But, she could hang with them.

"We'll see, won't we?" There were a few chuckles, and a couple of the guys ribbed him. She didn't say anything else. Actions spoke louder than words, after all.

The route was well marked, but Mitch still explained it to the recruits. It wrapped around the air field, ended where it began. "I'll follow along in the cart," Mitch said. "In case anyone needs first aid."

That was an excuse. Mitch hadn't run anywhere in years and everyone knew it. He'd suffered a fused disc in his back. He'd told her it was a struggle to keep his weight regulated.

They stepped up to the starting line. This was only a mile and a half, but she finished her stretches anyway, to set a good example. Sure enough, the guys followed her lead.

Finally, they lined up. "Go," Mitch said.

As she stepped into her first gaits, she inhaled what might have been her first full breath of the day. She stretched out, falling into a quick pace, but one that she assumed would give her under a seven-minute mile. It would be a hard standard for the recruits, but she figured that being one of the first across the finish would serve two purposes: she'd work off the tension and she'd prove to these guys that she had a right to be here.

Maybe she'd prove it to herself, too.

She pulled ahead of the pack. She'd started running shortly after her father's death. It had always been her escape. Today, she hoped it would help her leave her foolish attraction behind her.

With that thought, she sped up.

Chapter 5

Lance fell in step a few paces behind Meg. Together, they streaked along the course. He probably would have been able to catch her if he pushed hard—he was taller and a decent runner—but he didn't want to. She was on step to complete at least a seven-minute mile, and he didn't need to beat that to advance.

Besides, the view from here, with her auburn hair streaming behind her, her toned body…well, he didn't feel the need to win. Coming in second behind her would be just fine.

If he'd thought she was gorgeous before, watching her now, her body finely honed from what was obviously years of running, took his desire to a new level.

He wondered what had made her take up running. Meg hadn't played any sport when she was younger. Maybe he missed it, though, because he'd left before her sophomore year.

As if she sensed him behind her, she kicked up the speed as they neared the end. His lungs were screaming, but he kept up with her. They rushed across the finish line.

She slowed, checking her watch and pressing her other hand into the small of her back as she panted.

He stopped next to her, folding in half, his hands on his knees. He gasped out, "Damn, you're fast."

"Thanks." She glanced at her watch. "Good run."

He nodded. It was a good run for him, but her? She was amazing. "When did you get that fast?" He asked between breaths.

She shrugged, avoiding his eyes. He searched for something to say to smooth things over with her. The awkwardness…it was as if nothing had changed in the past ten years. If anything, it was worse.

Rock caught up with them, and she gave him his time. As they all caught their breath, waiting for the others, Rock glanced between them. "So," he said. "What's the story with you two?"

Meg tensed. "What do you mean?" Her voice was clipped, but maybe it was because she was out of breath.

"Dunno. You guys know each other or something?" Rock asked, his eyes narrowed.

"No," Meg said.

"Yes," Lance responded at the same time. He wasn't going to lie. When you came from a family with scandal in its history, lying only made things worse. If you were caught, it gave others fodder to believe everything bad about you.

No lies.

But if Meg didn't want to talk about it, he wasn't going to push. Not like everyone wasn't going to know the story in the end.

"Not anymore," she conceded, glaring at him.

The corner of Rock's mouth tilted up. "Right. Clears it all up."

Maybe this guy wasn't as dumb as he looked. Hid some brains behind his smart comments. He'd have to remember that.

Meg opened her mouth, presumably to explain, but Hunter and Dak trotted up, followed by Sledge and Digger. She snapped her mouth closed, checking her watch.

Only Kevin remained on the course, trudging along, nearing the finish line. Mitch followed him in the cart, barking. "Hurry up, son. You have twenty seconds."

Kevin pushed forward, as if digging deep for a burst of speed. He made it across the line with only a few seconds to go.

Mitch didn't celebrate. "That was sloppy. You think you're the tortoise? Slow and steady wins the race?" He called the recruits to line up, continuing his litany on Kevin. They stood quietly, listening.

Lance got it. Smokejumper standards were the highest, with good reason. There was only so much room on the planes they used. The available spaces needed to be filled with the best. If Kevin couldn't hack it, he didn't deserve to be here.

"Roberts." Mitch finally turned his attention to Lance.

"Sir."

"Good run. You almost caught her. Trust me, Meg's world class."

"She is, sir," he answered, his eyes finding Meg. She scowled at him.

"Since you all made it this far, it's time for the pack test." Mitch motioned to the air center. "Get set up. Your packs need to have 110 pounds in them. We leave in fifteen."

The other guys filed into the building, but Meg snagged his arm, holding him back. He glanced down at her fingers, and then lifted his eyebrows at her.

She immediately dropped her hand.

When they were alone, he smiled at her, clasping the back of his neck with his hands. Her gaze trailed across the span of his arms, and damned if her look of appreciation didn't make him feel ten feet tall. That she probably didn't want him to see her approval made his grin widen. "What can I do for you, Miss Buchanan?"

She glared at him. "You can knock it off."

"Knock what off?" he asked innocently.

"You know, Lance." Her brow wrinkled. "This is both of our jobs. Stop making it a joke."

That wiped the smile off his face. "This isn't a joke."

"Then why are you doing that?"

Though every self-preserving instinct screamed for him to stop, he closed the space between them, leaving only inches.

She sucked in a breath, though she probably didn't realize she did it. The slight inhalation struck him right in the chest. Her words were all bluster and defensiveness, but the way she responded...God, it did funny things to him. He refused to examine that too closely.

"What am I doing, Meg?" he asked, his voice low.

"You know what you're doing." Hers was a whisper. It made his blood heat. "Tell me."

She dropped her gaze to his chest and lifted her hands. "Stop. Please."

Even as she said the words, her eyes on him made him want to bury his hands in her hair, low on her neck, where her ponytail had loosened.

He didn't touch her, though. He promised he wouldn't and she said no. Still, he couldn't step away. Everything in him wailed for caution. The few inches between them were thick and his awareness of her thrummed.

Even as he wanted to be closer, he cursed himself. Pushing this was a bad idea, but he couldn't seem to help himself.

This couldn't be one-sided. She had to be having trouble being near him. He felt it, whatever beat between them. The intensity of it, the connection...

He massaged his chest, his brain scrambled.

She glared at him and waved at the air center. "Look what Rock said. He can tell we know each other."

"We do know each other."

She glared at him. "You know what I mean." The color was high on her cheeks, and he swallowed his groan. God, she was gorgeous all fired up.

"You're a recruit. I'm your trainer. If anyone even suspects that there's something unprofessional going on between us, we'd both be out of here." She pointed at him. "I've wanted this job for a long time. You're going to screw it up."

"Me? You're here, too, firecracker."

She rolled her eyes, folding her arms across her chest.

Looking at her was too hard, so he glanced at the building. He hated to admit it, but she was right. He hadn't been subtle. Rock had noticed there was something between them. If he was trying to protect her from whatever would come out about their fathers, he needed to keep things as focused on the job as possible.

This morning, his running shoes had been sliced open. He'd needed to duct tape them for training today, until he could get out to buy a new pair. No one had said anything. Maybe the rest of them thought this was how he liked his shoes. But, someone was trying to tell him he wasn't wanted.

None of that was stuff he wanted her near.

"Okay. Fine. I can be professional." He hoped. Her lips split into a triumphant grin, so he must have been believable. "But, in return, I want something from you."

"What?" Wariness clouded her face. He didn't like how it looked on her features.

"I want you to give me a chance."

"A chance?" Her gaze hardened. "I told you I wouldn't get in your way here. You'll have a fair chance."

"Not just a chance in training, a chance to not be enemies." He sighed. "I know we can't be friends. Not anymore. But I'd at least like us not to be enemies."

"You aren't my enemy." She didn't meet his eyes, glancing over his shoulder as if checking to make sure no one heard them.

"Then why were you so quick to pretend we don't know each other?" he challenged. "You would have owned a former acquaintance. That's more than I got."

"Come on, Lance. This is hard."

He was pushing her too far. But he hated being some dirty secret. And maybe if he could get through to her now, when she found out his secret, it might help.

It was the best he could hope for.

He smiled his most persuasive grin. "This way, we both get what we want. You get me on my best behavior and maybe I get to not be someone you hate anymore."

"I don't hate you." She propped her hands on her hips and glanced over his shoulder, toward the air center, her brow creased. "Fine."

"Fine, what?"

"I'll…" She bit her lip, rolling her eyes to the heavens as if looking for guidance. "I'll give you a chance, as long as you don't get us both fired."

He smothered his grin. "Deal."

"You need to do better," she reiterated.

This time, he couldn't stop his chuckle. "Firecracker, I told you. You're safe from me." He wouldn't admit how much he wished he hadn't made that promise, even though it served his purposes here. "From now on, I'm on my best behavior."

She nodded. Turning, she walked into the building and he watched her go, the grin slipping from his face.

He had years of experience pretending that he didn't want her. He was at expert level.

As he followed her in, he tried to ignore how much it bothered him that he'd need to go back to that…pretending. Now that he'd allowed his attraction free reins, trying to stuff it back inside him was almost painful.

He'd done hard things before. He could do this.

Joining the others, he hurried now to get his pack together. Nearby, Meg drank from her water bottle. He paused to watch, fascinated by the tilt of her neck, the vulnerable curve of her collar bone.

Dropping his gaze, he forced himself to look away. As he jammed heavy stuff in his pack, trying to get to the required weight, he wondered how many times he'd need to rip his gaze from her in the coming days.

More than a few, he guessed.

* * * *

As Meg waited for the rookies to return from their pack test, she tried not to be nervous or wonder what Lance meant by "a chance."

To her, it sounded a lot like a chance to get under her skin.

Could she blame him, though? If the roles were reversed, she wouldn't want to be the town pariah. Maybe he hoped she would help him mend fences with Hunter. That would go a long way to easing his return home.

Except, she had no idea how she would try to be friends—friendly professionals—with him. Not when every time she saw him, she couldn't stop noticing how he moved, how he smelled, how her body craved him.

As she staked out a spot near the door she expected them to come in, she tried to pretend she wasn't waiting for them. It was a fine line between looking busy and trying not to look like she was looking busy.

Dak and Hunter filed in first, dragging their packs and gear. They looked tired, hot, but also relieved. This was the last task in the physical test. They'd both passed and would move on to the next phase. While the physical tests were the minimum requirements and most of the recruits could easily pass, there was stress attached to it. Walking into a new job and having to pass an exam on the first day? She bet they were happy it was over.

Her pride swelled. She'd assumed her brother would pass, but she never got sick of watching him succeed.

If he'd been alone, she would have congratulated him. Except Dak was with him. For all the mental pep talks, she wasn't ready to join them, not as their trainer. She'd have been fine stepping forward as his sister. Her brother definitely belonged here. Without Mitch, though, she felt out of place.

Which was ridiculous. This was her job. She should congratulate them. Being here, in Redmond, at the air center, had shaken her confidence. This tentative woman…this wasn't who she was.

Decided, she stepped forward, to talk to them. That's when she overheard their conversation.

"You know Lance." Her brother's voice was deceptively mild.

Dak grunted. "Yeah. We worked together in California." He continued unpacking his gear, ignoring Hunter. Hunter didn't let it go, though.

"California, huh?" Hunter threw his pack into his locker. "You grow up there?"

"No." Dak didn't expand.

"Why come here?"

She scowled. There was some level of animosity toward outsiders among the local hotshot crews, but she hadn't expected it from her brother.

"California." Dak snorted. "All those sandy beaches, the sun…. Sucks."

She smothered her laugh. It was the perfect response. It pointed out that Hunter was being nosy without directly calling him out.

Hunter snorted, didn't respond. There was a pause, and she stepped closer, to see them. From her vantage point on the threshold of Mitch's office, she watched both men unpacking, neither looking at the other.

"Lance is from Redmond. He's got history here."

"I hear." Dak wasn't giving him anything. Her brother was being rude. Her respect for Dak grew.

Hunter stood then, facing the other man. "Be careful. Knowing him here won't do you any favors."

Meg stifled her gasp. What the hell was Hunter doing? Was that a threat? A warning? He should have kept his mouth shut. They'd talked about this yesterday. They agreed that Lance deserved a fair shot.

This was a low blow.

Dak straightened, and the two men sized each other up. Dak's jaw firmed, and whatever he was about to say would draw a line between them. It was all over his face.

Dak shouldn't have to defend anyone. She stepped into the doorway. "Hunter," she snapped. "That's enough."

Her brother's chin notched up and his eyes flashed. He didn't like to be chastised and she bet he hated that she did it in front of a fellow recruit. But what could he say? She was their trainer, an authority figure, and they both knew it. Spinning away, he returned to his unpacking.

As if her body could sense him where he was, she turned to find Lance in the doorway.

He didn't say anything. Maybe he hadn't heard the exchange. The intensity of his gaze bored into her, saying he'd heard enough. She opened her mouth, but what could she say?

To cover her discomfort, she nodded to Dak.

The rest of the recruits filed past her and Lance, breaking the tension, allowing her to retreat. As Mitch joined them and the rookies panted, sweaty and tired, he checked his watch. "It's only noon, gentlemen. Time for PT."

Without another word, he walked into the office. They'd all passed, then.

Which meant the real training began. They didn't get time to snack, not even time to rehydrate. This was smokejumper training. These men needed to be pushed to the edge of their endurance, because if they were expected to parachute into a fire, and then walk back out when they were done fighting it, they needed to be tested.

And testing is what she'd do.

They all hurried around, dropping their packs, getting into training clothes. They looked tired, but exhilarated. Lance nodded to her before he followed the rest of them without another word.

As they dispersed, she tailed Hunter as he headed toward the bunkhouse. No matter what happened in the past, Lance didn't deserve to be treated like this. She caught up with her brother in the hall, shoving him on the arm. "What the hell was that?"

Her brother folded his arms over his chest, his sullenness similar to what she saw on the twins' faces sometimes. "What?"

"You were a jerk. That was stupid."

"It was all true. He wasn't a good friend to me. Felt the guy could use a warning." He shrugged, unconcerned.

She blinked at him. "Grow up, Hunter."

Her brother's face sharpened with pain for a moment before it closed up again. He trudged to the door, shouldering it open to go outside.

First Will, now Hunter. Lance didn't deserve that. When their fathers died, they'd been kids. They hadn't been given directions on how to survive the events of that day or their grief. They'd done the best they could.

That wasn't enough anymore.

Lance was right. She wasn't sure if she could be a friend to him, didn't even know if she could be friendly, not with how attracted she was to him still. But, she could do this. She could smooth things over with her brothers, give him the chance he'd asked for.

Convinced, she returned to her office and jotted a note and her cell phone number on a Post-it. The main room outside was bustling with recruits and seasoned jumpers here to train. In the hustle of it all, she drifted to Lance's locker space. She dropped the Post-it into his street shoes.

Hopefully he'd get it, or she'd need to find another way to get into contact with him.

Uncertainty gripped her. Spending extra time with Lance was a stupid idea. The more she was with him, the more she wanted to be with him.

She could do this, though. For Lance and for Hunter. They'd been best friends. If she could help them find that again, it was worth it.

If it brought one of her brothers some peace after all these years, she'd do anything.

* * * *

"Are you sure you can drop me at the bar?" Dak threw his jacket into the backseat of the Jeep before climbing into the passenger side. "I can stay here. In fact, I should do that."

Lance slid into the driver's seat and jammed the key in the ignition. "I was going out anyway. No biggie."

Dak grunted, grumbling under his breath about how he hated people.

"Stop it. No you don't. Get in." Starting the engine, he smiled at his friend. "Look at you, going out for beers with the guys. When did you become such a joiner?" In California, Dak had never gone out of his way to make friends, kept to himself. Lance didn't take no, though. He'd nagged, teased, bullied the guy into befriending him. There was a story there, Lance was positive, but Dak kept it to himself. Lance let him. It didn't matter. He'd always been a loyal friend, and that was good enough for Lance.

Dak punched him in the shoulder. "Shut up." But he chuckled. "It's a good strategy. I need to work with these guys. It won't kill me to have a drink with them."

"A good strategy? What are you, a robot?" Lance glanced at him as he navigated the turn onto the road into town, shifting the Jeep into a higher gear. "And I don't know about that. It sounds painful. Sledge is kind of a dickhead."

"Always one in every crowd. You should know."

Lance barked a laugh. "Nice."

"So where are you going instead of joining our little gathering? And, can you take me with you?"

Lance's mouth thinned, and he cast another look at Dak. He wasn't sure he should share. He didn't know what was happening with Meg, but whatever it was he'd prefer to keep it close to the vest.

At the end of the day, when he'd returned to his locker to grab his stuff, he'd found a note from her in his shoes.

Let's talk. Text me. It had listed her number and been signed only with an M.

His heart in his throat, he'd sent her a quick message right there, sweating in front of his locker. *Meet you at Stack Park. Half hour?*

Sure.

He knew he shouldn't meet up with the trainer—it wouldn't look good—but he could trust Dak. He deserved the truth.

"I'm headed to see Meg Buchanan." He twisted the steering wheel in his hand.

Dak whistled low. "You think that's a good idea? Hanging out with our trainer, away from work?"

He shrugged. "We're old friends. She asked to see me, that's all. Completely innocent."

The pause that filled the Jeep was empty, as if Dak left it there for Lance to fill up. Finally, he said, "I'm trying to mend fences."

"Tell yourself that lie. I don't believe that shit." Dak breathed out. "I see the way you look at her. Everyone does."

Lance pursed his lips, but he didn't respond. He didn't doubt Dak at all. If he didn't curb his staring at her, he'd give himself away completely.

"Be careful. That's all."

He grunted. "I can handle myself."

"No, not you. Her." Dak's voice was serious. "Does she know you want to look into your father's death?"

He shook his head. Damn it. That was the problem with good friends. They could poke you in the softest spots.

"I thought so."

"It hasn't exactly come up in conversation. 'Hi, I know this might be hard for you, but by the way, I'm trying to clear my dad's name and I'll be digging into our families' histories. Hope that's okay.'" Lance snorted. "Please. I just got here. Give me some time to smooth things over before I talk to her about it."

"Did you plan to do that?"

Lance cringed.

Dak exhaled. "I thought so." He exhaled. "You care for her. It's obvious. So be careful."

Lance pulled into a parking spot in front of the bar. Everything was already complicated enough. Dak was right, after all. He hated him pointing it out, but he couldn't refute it. So he did what he always did when he had no comeback: he made a joke.

He shifted into park, and reached over to ruffle Dak's hair. "Go play nice now. Don't forget your manners."

"Thanks, Mom." Dak shook his head and gave him the finger. Lance laughed, and they let it go.

Reaching behind them, Dak grabbed his jacket. Lance pulled his own bag from the back and dropped it onto the seat beside him. A blank envelope slipped out of the open zipper.

Lance snapped it up, showing it to Dak through the window. "Is this yours?"

He shook his head. "Nah. I only brought my jacket. What is it?"

Lance slipped his finger under the fold and pulled out a single sheet of paper. It only had two typed sentences on the page.

You aren't wanted. Watch your back.

He handed the page to his friend who read it with a glance. "What the hell?"

"I don't know." He took the page back, reading it again though the words were already burned in his memory. "I didn't see anyone near my stuff. Whoever put that in there must've done it earlier today, when I wasn't around."

Dak leaned in the open window, resting on his elbows, his voice low. "That's messed up. Would only be creepier is if it was made out of cut out letters from a magazine or something."

"Yeah. You're right." He couldn't take his eyes off the six words in front of him. *Watch your back, watch your back...*

First his sneakers this morning, now this.

Did someone know he was looking for information about his father? Is that why he was being threatened?

The first part...that he wasn't wanted. That sounded like sour grapes, not concern that he was investigating. He loosened his grip on the paper. Whoever had written this, it didn't sound like they were upset about him looking for information.

Good. It would be better if no one knew he was searching for answers. Doors would close.

"Are you going to show it to Joe? Seems like something he should know."

Lance tore his head from the page. He refolded the letter, tucking it back into the envelope. "So he can make things weird in the air center, make this harder for me than it already is? No. The best thing to do is to ignore it." He opened the glove box, tucked the note on top of his car manual and insurance card, and slammed it shut.

Besides, he didn't need more eyes on him. The closer they watched him, the less he could find out.

"I don't know..."

"This is some prank. Someone's trying to scare me, break my concentration. That's all. I'm not going to let some note freak me out." He gripped the steering wheel tighter, his resolve firming. "I'm sure it's nothing."

Dak patted the door, pushing away. "If you say so, man. But I would be careful. Keep your eyes open."

Lance offered him his best cocky grin. "Always." He shifted to drive as Dak stepped back.

"And Lance?"

"Yeah?"

"I'm here, if you need me."

At any other time, Lance might have made some smart comment, razzing his friend for being overly cautious, but right now with a threatening letter in his glove box, he couldn't work up the proper bravado. Instead, he nodded. "Thanks."

Dak saluted and stepped onto the curve outside the bar. As Lance pulled away, he lifted a hand. Lance waved back

As he headed toward the park to meet Meg, he couldn't keep himself from glancing at the glove compartment.

Chapter 6

The sun was setting as Lance pulled into an empty parking spot at Stack Park. Killing the engine, he grabbed the sandwiches he'd picked up on the way before climbing out of the Jeep.

Across the park, he spotted Meg sitting at a picnic table. Her shoulders hunched and her head down, she leaned forward on her knees with her hands folded together. Even from this far, he could sense her apprehension. It tugged at his gut that they'd come to this. That she would be anxious about meeting with him.

Pausing, he reached into the backseat of the Jeep and grabbed the hoodie he'd tossed there earlier. Then he slammed the door and hit the lock button. Best not to keep it open with that letter in the glove box. The Jeep beeped, and he set off toward her, yanking the zipper on his fleece up higher under his chin.

Traipsing through the dusk light, he grinned. He hadn't sneaked out to meet a girl at night since high school.

And that girl hadn't been as amazing as Meg Buchanan.

He trotted over a few jutting tree roots and around a cropping of rocks, wincing. Damn. Everything ached. They'd spent the afternoon training. He'd known the physical requirements of smokejumping would be strenuous, but no one could really prepare for the muscle exhaustion that came from almost ten hours of straight physical activity. They'd done two more runs and so many calisthenics he'd lost count.

That was going to hurt tomorrow.

Seeing him coming, Meg sat up and wrapped her arms around her middle. She wore the same tracksuit he'd seen her in earlier. She could wear a sack and look gorgeous to him, but the outfit wasn't warm enough for the cool spring night. He offered the sweatshirt he'd grabbed to her. "Here."

"No, no...I'm fine." She shook her head.

"You're shivering." He shook it. "Take it."

He watched her decide whether it was more important to be stubborn or to be warm. Comfort won.

As she pulled the garment on and it swallowed her slight frame, he tried to ignore how good she looked wearing his clothes. He lifted the food bags. "I also brought dinner."

She wrapped her arms around herself, smiling. "I didn't even think about food."

The statement was so telling it tugged at his heart. Her position, the absence of a coat...she was upset. He didn't know exactly why, but he could guess that it had something to do with him.

That made his resolve to smooth things over with her even stronger.

He'd decided, after his conversation with her this morning, that he was going to find a way to be make this easier for her, for her family. He didn't know how, exactly, and even the suggestion that he could accept being friends with her without wanting more was ridiculous. But he was going to try.

It wouldn't be easy. He planned to find out what happened with his father, and he figured that was going to be...difficult. And he wasn't leaving training, so if it was his presence—the reminder of how his family had caused chaos in hers—was getting to her, he couldn't do much about that.

Still, he could go a long way to mending fences. Maybe they could never get back to where they used to be, but they had been friends before. He had his hopes they'd find that again.

Starting now.

He plopped the bag on the table, reaching into the sack, determined to keep the mood light. "After the way you drove us today? You really are a slave driver." He shuffled the contents as he asked, "When did you start running?"

She shrugged. "After Dad died, I couldn't sleep, and things were hard at the house. I started to go for runs. I got good at it." She didn't go on.

There were so many things he could say or ask. What got hard? Learning she couldn't sleep...he wanted to know why. Except years of silence remained between them. As he tried to find a way around it, the moment passed.

He lifted a sandwich from the bag. "I got subs. Yours is dry. That's still how you like it, right?"

She blinked. "You remember that?"

Damn it. He did his best not to squirm under her gaze. Had he given himself away that easily? This "friends" endeavor might be short-lived. To smooth over the tell, he shrugged. "Sure. I remember stuff like that."

That was true enough. In fact, it was one of his foibles. Details. He remembered how people took their coffee, how they liked their sandwiches. If they preferred a certain brand of chips, if they didn't like ice in their drinks. Things like that stayed with him.

It was his best excuse. The real reason? He doubted he'd forgotten anything about her over the years. Didn't think he could if he wanted to. That would remain his secret.

"I know you do."

He paused, his hand inside the brown bag. Did she remember that about him, then? Did she remember other things about him, too?

Didn't matter if she remembered anything, did it? Friends. That was his goal. He yanked out the wrapped sandwiches, setting them out, and removed a bunch of napkins. He added the two bags of chips and the drinks he'd snagged. It was a strange habit. That was the only reason she remembered.

"So tell me. From the way you ran us ragged today, you can obviously pull your weight. How come you never took up firefighting?" He chuckled. "Obviously you have the pedigree."

His laughter died when he caught her face. She was pale—paler than usual—in the dim light. "I tried. A few years ago."

He cocked his head. "You did?"

She nodded. "Yeah. Let's just say firefighting stopped being something on my to-do list."

He couldn't even remember a time when they hadn't talked about becoming firefighters. That there were female smokejumpers had cemented it in Meg's mind back then. She insisted that it wouldn't matter that she was smaller, thinner. She could hold her own on a crew, she'd said. He'd believed her. Now, after watching her train all day, it was clear she was right.

What had changed that? He opened her mouth to ask, but her next words stopped him.

"You were right." She twisted, tucking her legs under the picnic table. Tilting her head back, she studied him, her face devoid of the defensiveness he'd come to expect from her the past couple of days. With her hair in a ponytail and the late-day light hitting her face, she reminded him more of the girl she'd been years ago. He'd found that girl tempting and appealing. This woman…he found her irresistible. "About how you needed a chance."

"I am?" He glanced down, unwrapping the sandwiches. "Is that why you brought me out here?" He grinned at her. "I could have saved you a trip. I'm usually right."

"Ha." She smiled back. "No, I mean after the way Hunter acted today, it's pretty clear you're right. You do need my help."

He took a bite of his sandwich, stalling while he figured out a response.

He'd wondered if she'd bring that up. He walked in on the tail end of that conversation. *Knowing him here won't do you any favors.* What did that even mean? Sure, this was a small community, a tight-knit one, and it had a long memory.

But of all the people he'd expected to judge him, he hadn't picked Hunter. They'd been so close before everything went down. So close, that afterward, he'd been unable to face him. Between how broken up Hunter's mom had been, how distant Lance's had become, and how the rest of Redmond had made them into pariahs...he couldn't have handled any of that from Hunter. Later, after he'd gotten some distance and time away, he'd realized what a shit he'd been. Hunt was his best friend. He'd deserved an explanation. Instead, he'd been afraid that if he started talking to Hunter about it, if his friend had shown any animosity, he'd break down, cry like a baby. He'd chosen to be proud.

That had been a mistake.

That didn't explain how Hunter acted today. Why had he talked to Dak? If nothing else, he had to know that would cause a rift in the class. No one wanted enemies. What had he been trying to prove?

"I'll talk to Hunter." It was past time. He'd avoided the conversation when they were teenagers, but now, as a man, he could see that had been a mistake. He'd known then it was a mistake. He'd only been too afraid to fix it.

"Let me help you. That's what you wanted, right?" She pulled her sandwich toward her. "You and Hunter used to be inseparable. You want that back. He does, too. Even if he's acting like an ass right now."

Watching her with narrowed eyes, he tried to piece together what she was trying to say. "You're going to help me with Hunter."

"You need it, right?" She shrugged. "I'll see what I can do."

He blinked, not sure what to say. This was an easy way out. If she believed he only needed her to help him smooth things over with her family, with the community, then he could hide behind that.

So why was he so pissed?

As he watched her pick up her sandwich and find the best approach to dig in, he figured it out. It bothered him that she didn't consider that he'd wanted the chance with just *her*.

Except he shouldn't be thinking that at all.

Unaware of his internal struggle, she bit into her sandwich, pausing to chew, before using it to point at him. "This is good. I forgot how good Rozele's is." She wiped her mouth with a napkin, and tucked it under her drink so it didn't blow away. "Give him some time. He'll come around."

"Is that what you've been doing for the past years? Giving each other some time?" That was harsh. Some part of him recognized that he was lashing out, that it was unfair.

She glared at him, her sandwich halted on its way to her mouth. "What's that supposed to mean?"

Did she even notice that there was something stiff and unnatural between her and her siblings? He'd grown up with them. They'd always had an easy way among them. They joked, poked fun. Stuck up for each other. Now, they were formal. Like strangers.

It wasn't his place to say anything, though. Not anymore, and especially not in his current mood. "Never mind."

"No, what do you mean?"

"You guys. You're all different now." It was an understatement. Her brothers were so serious, he hardly recognized them. When he looked into Hunter's face, he couldn't even find his old partner in crime.

And Meg? She was so buttoned up he couldn't help missing the girl who tagged along on their escapades.

"We lost our father, Lance," she said stiffly. "Of course, we're different."

"Forget it." Why was he picking this fight? He wanted to smooth things over with her.

She placed her sandwich on its wrapper, took a sip of her iced tea, and rubbed the dust from her finger tips. "No. You started this. Let's get it out."

They were going to do this now, it seemed.

So be it.

"Hunter's never been that quiet. The guy never shut up. And Will might have been overbearing and obnoxious, but the way he acted yesterday? That was a whole new level. That was past overbearing, right to downright dickish."

She snorted, the side of her lip tilting up.

"Is that a smile?" He leaned back, lifting his hands. "My job here is done, folks."

Sighing, she shook her head. "They've had a hard time." Her grin faded, and he was sad to see it go. The worry that replaced it, the faraway look… it was new, unfamiliar on Meg's face. It tugged at his heart.

"What about you, Megs?" he asked softly.

"What about me?" She glanced down at her sandwich, as if it suddenly became incredibly interesting, even though she'd been having a hard time getting into it.

"How are you doing?" He leaned forward, doing his best to see her, to study her in the light from the rising moon. Her hair shimmered, and her skin looked so soft he wanted to run his thumb along her cheekbone. She wouldn't welcome that, but that didn't stop him from wanting.

"I'm fine." The answer came fast, gave nothing away, and was complete bullshit.

"I don't believe you. I think you hold it together, hold your family together, because there's no one else to do it. You have to be strong for everyone. And while you're being strong, no one's there to be strong for you." He'd rarely regretted leaving Redmond. His mom had been miserable in the months after his father's death, and he'd wanted to see her happy. The relief had been intense the first months after they'd gone. He'd ignored any pangs of homesickness in those first days, relieved to see his mother smile again.

After things settled, though, the lack of closure, the sense of unease, it had settled over him.

This, though…never had he expected Meg to be holding her family together.

She swallowed, holding his gaze. Obviously, he was right. Always the one to make peace. Of course, she would step in to make things easier for everyone else. It was one of the things he'd always loved about her, how selfless she was.

But that didn't mean they should have let her. Who had taken care of her? She hadn't been able to sleep? Had turned to running to make it bearable? That was messed up.

Anger burned through him…at Hunter, at Will. Hadn't they noticed? How had they not seen how much the strain was tearing at her? If they saw it, why weren't they doing anything about it?

They'd left so much unsaid, all of them. And it looked like Meg had picked up all the slack.

He didn't think he'd ever met anyone as loyal as her. Her devotion to her family, to the people she loved…it was one of the sexiest things about her.

"You're wrong." She looked down, dropping her eyes. Picking up her sandwich, she took another bite. After she finished chewing, she glanced up. By then, she'd gone into hiding and everything he'd seen in her eyes a minute ago was gone. "You've got it wrong. I only did what I had to do. My family needed me."

He bet they had. He would bring that up to her brothers sometime soon, whether they wanted to hear it or not. "I hear your mom is still having a hard time."

"Who told you that?" Her brows snapped together. "You haven't been home that long." She might have been uncomfortable talking about her brothers or herself but now that he brought up her mom, she'd come to battle.

Maybe he should have kept his mouth shut. "My grandmother said your mom has had a hard time. That's all."

"That's none of her business." She glared at him. "It's hard to be a single mom. The twins are teenagers; they're a handful. And she works full time."

"I know." He didn't say more. He'd watched his own mother struggle with life after his father's death. His dad had been the life and laughter in their house, at least during the times he was home. There had been a vacuum his naturally introverted mother hadn't been able to fill.

But, after a year or so, she'd stretched out. She'd let go of some of their old habits and they started new traditions in Mendocino. His mother purchased a bed and breakfast. He'd volunteered at the fire company, and after high school, he'd joined the hotshot crew in Stonyford.

He didn't see his mom's B&B as home, but she was happy. She'd remarried a couple years ago to a nice man with laugh lines around his eyes, Ollie. Lance had spent the weeks before rookie training in Mendocino, at his mom's place.

From what he could tell, Meg's mom hadn't made any changes. She'd gotten stuck.

She placed her hands on the table, as if she was going to get up. "You don't know what happened after you left. It was hard. Don't judge."

He didn't want her to leave. "You're right. I don't know what happened after I left. Things were hard for us, too. But that was ten years ago. Some of it is better now, some remains."

It didn't look like any of it was better for the Buchanans.

"There's no time limit on some things." She cringed, and again the years between them stretched wide. Ten years was a long time, but it wasn't long enough to get past unsaid things. Reality needed to be voiced, whether it was convenient or not.

"I should have come to see you all, after everything. I didn't, and I wish I had." It was the truth. It felt good to say it.

"Yes. You should have. Hunter…" She shook her head. "Hunter missed you."

The words cut through him. "I missed him, too." He met her gaze. "I missed all of you."

"Then what the hell, Lance?" She pushed her sandwich away and pinned him with a glare. "Hunter called you. He texted. You had to have gotten at least a few of those messages."

"I did."

"Then why didn't you reach out?" Her voice was raw. "We were all broken. You could have been broken with us."

This was awful, so much harder than he'd ever expected. He'd known, when he returned to Redmond, that he couldn't avoid these conversations, not if he was going to become a smokejumper, not if he was going to try to clear his father's name. But, her eyes...they were full of pain.

"Christ, Meg. I wanted to." He ran his hands over his hair. "You have no idea how many times I wanted to come over, to see all of you. Every time...I'd lose my nerve." Or he'd see someone who would shake his resolve. The neighbors. A teacher. The man at the deli who always served them. Everyone.

"He could have used your help." She leaned back. "I didn't know how to reach him. Still don't."

He wanted to reach for her hand. But that stupid promise not to touch her stopped him. Stupid or not, he refused to renege on it. So, he said the words he needed to say.

"I'm sorry, Meg." He shook his head. "I couldn't." Back then, he couldn't reach out. Even as the loss of his friends was like a physical pain, a secondary blow to the loss of his father, he'd been paralyzed. Even now, years later, that boy shamed him.

The sun had set completely now, and there was barely any light, but her blue gaze filled his sight. He refused to break the contact.

This had been a bad idea. He'd wanted to call a truce, a new start with her. Something to build on, so that maybe he could explain what he was doing here, investigating their fathers' deaths. If they were friends, he could explain that knowing the full truth about their fathers would be right, in the end. For that to happen, she would need to see him as something other than the son of the man who killed her dad, something more than the friend who'd abandoned them all years ago.

That's the lie he'd told himself. He'd wanted to start fresh with *her*, to get another chance to have her in his life.

He could see now that would be impossible.

She stood, shaking her head. "Thank you. For dinner and everything. I should get back."

He lifted his hand, reaching for her. But the space across the table held a lifetime. He couldn't span it. "Meg..."

"And Lance?"

He swallowed. "Yeah?"

"I'll do as you asked. Help you with Hunter, give you a chance here as best I can. But, we can't be friends. Goodnight."

He didn't go after her as she headed toward her SUV.

The sandwich he'd eaten sat like a stone in his gut, coated in disappointment. He'd hoped that if he could smooth over some of the pain, he'd be able to convince Meg and her brothers that reopening the investigation into their fathers' deaths would benefit them all. As she drove out of the parking lot, she took any dreams of that possibility with her.

Chapter 7

Meg pulled in behind her mom's Explorer, killing the engine. The house was dark except for the light they left on over the kitchen window and the faint glow from the living room. She allowed her head to sag and closed her eyes.

What had she been doing, thinking she could help Lance smooth things over? To do that, she would have needed to be able to get past her own mixed up baggage about him. Which she'd believed she could. She was a grown-up now, paid her own bills, had a successful career, friends, and life. She could handle her emotions.

Wrong.

All those questions, poking and prodding. Like he was trying to dig up all the stuff she'd buried.

Shaking her head, she grabbed her purse and duffel out of the passenger seat. She slammed the door harder than necessary and trudged up the stairs. The screen door closed with a bang behind her.

"Meg? Is that you?" Her mom's voice wafted from the living room.

Damn. She'd hoped to miss her. "Yeah."

"I was just going to watch my story. Care to join me?"

Meg's eyes closed. Small talk with her mother sounded like torture. She needed to retreat to her room and get some sleep, so she could put her guard back up tomorrow. But, she mustered a smile as she dropped her bags on the ground next to the cluttered table.

In the living room, her mom was already in her pajamas, curled up on the love seat, with her favorite flannel blanket over her legs. Her fuzzy slippers stuck out the bottom. In a messy bun and her face free of makeup, she looked younger. Seeing her like this made Meg wonder what she would've been like if her father hadn't died. Would she be the same shell of a woman she was now? Or would she be the energetic mother of her youth?

It was probably somewhere in the middle. No one stayed the same after ten years. Some things got better, some things worse…. Like her. Like Lance.

A takeout container sat open on the coffee table next to her, the remains of what had probably been Chinese food. "Where are the boys?"

"I dropped them at Kyle's an hour or so ago." Her mom set her glass next to the remains of her dinner. "Some 'Call of Duty' tournament or something."

Meg nodded as she picked up the trash, closing the lid. Still antsy, she returned to the kitchen and dropped it into the garbage can. "How was your day?"

"Same." Her mom shrugged, and her face split into a half grin. "Nothing much changes at urgent care. How was your day? How are things going at the air center?" The question was mild, guarded. They both knew her mom didn't want to know what happened at the air center.

"Fine." They were talking but they weren't saying anything.

Meg dropped into the recliner next to the couch. Elbows on knees, she rested her face in her hands.

These kinds of conversations…pointless. After every talk she'd had with Will, Hunter, and now Lance, it was clear that no one was better off by everything they left unsaid. She was angry. She hadn't known that until tonight. There was no other explanation for why she hadn't accepted Lance's apology. And it made her even more mad to be controlled by something she didn't understand.

She inhaled a deep breath. "Lance Roberts is back." She tried to ignore the stiffening of her mom's back, forging ahead. "He's in this year's recruit class. With Hunter. Did you know?"

"No. I didn't." Her mom scooted back, sitting up. "What the hell was Joe thinking? He should know better." Her forehead firmed, emphasizing the creases that had become more prominent over the past decade.

"You sound like Will and Hunter." It sounded like an accusation. Maybe it was. Lance didn't deserve this reaction. "And why would he know better? As far as I can see, he wasn't in that plane with Dad. He has as much right to be there as the rest of them."

Her mom's mouth fell open, and her eyes widened. "You have to be kidding."

"It's been long enough. Lance spent the past ten years doing the same things Hunter has. Volunteering, working on a hotshot crew, helitack. He's not different."

"The Roberts men…" Mom folded her arms over her chest, her knuckles white on her sleeves. "They're dangerous."

"Lance was like another son to you."

Her mom swallowed and when she spoke again, it was softer. "You didn't grow up with JT. He was reckless, took unnecessary risk."

"No, but I grew up with Will, Hunt, and Lance. I know about unnecessary risk."

Her mother's eyes narrowed. "I can't believe I have to explain this to you. JT is the reason your father is dead."

"He was never formally accused. It was an accident." She had no idea why she was pushing this, especially tonight when she was already so raw.

"An accident thanks to a whole bunch of careless mistakes."

"What mistakes?" Meg asked, but she wasn't sure she wanted to know.

Her mom shook her head. "You don't need to hear this. It was hard enough on all of you."

"It's still hard, Mom. Can't you see that? Nothing has changed." Meg's voice was a whisper. "Don't you think I deserve the truth?"

Her mother's eyes were hard, boring into her. Silently, they stared at each other. Meg breathed hard, her fist clenched. She didn't want to fight, not with her mother, but the frustration from talking to Lance, from arguing with her brothers…it was too close to the surface, boiling over.

Her mom looked away first. She sighed, and her voice was small when she spoke. "JT talked your father into going to the most dangerous side of the flames, but then he convinced him to stay there, battle the blaze from that flank. Joe said that when he told them to back up, to get away… it was Lance's father who convinced Jason to stay. That they were making progress. Joe gave up and left them, and it probably saved his life. He set up a fire shelter away from danger." She glanced back at Meg. "They found your father and Lance's under a shelter too close to the flames."

Meg had heard bits and pieces of this story over the years. The part about how they were on the wrong side of the fire, how they were together under one shelter, and how the flames had gotten too hot where they were set up.

Where was the rest of the detail, though? "How can you be sure any of that was Mr. Roberts' fault?"

"They have a recording, of him convincing your father to jump. Joe said that JT lost his shelter or ripped it or something. He didn't have it. So your father had to share his with JT. Maybe if they'd had that, they could both have protected themselves." Her mouth twisted. "Instead, your father sacrificed himself, to try to save him."

Meg covered her mouth with her fingers. Good God. The details…

"Stay away from him." Her mother shifted, swinging her legs over the side of the couch and staring at her dead on. "You know Lance. He's like his father. Reckless, careless. For your own good, stay away."

She got up then, leaving Meg alone with the images in her head.

Her mom's warning was crystal clear. This wasn't about Lance paying for the sins of his father. It was that he was like him in so many ways. Charismatic, full of swagger. Even if he didn't deserve to be judged by his father's past, he was fully capable of making his mistakes in the present.

She didn't believe that crap. No one got to choose their family. Apparently, her mom didn't agree.

This was too much, too hard.

He asked for a chance, but being his friend would only lead to heartache. She already had no self-control where he was concerned. She would help him fix his friendship with Hunter, and then she'd leave him alone.

Lance Roberts was a complication she couldn't afford.

* * * *

When Lance's phone vibrated later that night, after he was already settled in to his bed at the air center, he swept it up and hurried out the side door. The phone had only been inches away, because he didn't want it to get stolen like his workout gear had been. When he'd returned from Stack Park, it had all been gone. Just another entertaining prank, apparently. He put as much distance between himself and any prying ears as he could before he answered. "Thanks for returning my call, sir."

"Not at all, son. I've heard you're back in Redmond. Welcome home." Roger Palance's gruff voice hadn't changed over the past ten years. Smoker's lung with a side of grumpy grandfather.

"Thank you." That was as good of an opening as he was going to get. "That's why I was calling. I hoped I could pay you a visit. Catch up on old times."

Lance propped his free hand on his hip, staring up at the starry sky. This was an overreach. He and Palance hadn't been close, and in fact Palance hadn't even liked his father, if the rumors were true. Said he was cocky, which was true. But, he had something Lance needed, and in his experience, most people weren't rude enough to deny requests from an old dead friend's son.

"Old times, huh?" Palance's chuckle rumbled over the line. "What old times would that be?"

Good question. Their families hadn't been close. "Had a few things I'd like to talk to you about, that's all."

"Seems we're talking just fine right now." If Lance didn't know any better, he'd guess the old guy was having a good time.

This wasn't going to work. Palance was too perceptive. Time to get to the point. "I wanted to talk about my father."

The chuckle vibrated over the line. "I figured."

"You were the pilot on my father's last flight. I hoped you could answer a few questions for me."

"Think I answered a lot of questions back then. Investigators, law enforcement. Professionals. What new questions could a kid have after all these years?"

He could picture the sort of interrogation Palance had withstood. He'd been one of the last people to talk to the deceased. But it had been a decade since he'd been a kid. "I can understand your frustration. I'm only trying to get a bigger picture. My mom gave me the investigator's official report, but..."

"But you wanted to check his work."

"No." Lance exhaled. "Yes. Maybe." Is that what he was doing? The report didn't make sense. On paper, he understood. His father was overheard convincing Jason Buchanan to follow him. But why? His father had been jumping fires for years. No way he'd misread the burn so thoroughly.

Yet that's what happened. Somehow Jason, Joe, and his dad ended up on the wrong side of the fire, with only two shelters. Then, the newbie came home alive while the seasoned veterans—each with over ten years of experience—were caught in the flames. It didn't add up. His dad was reckless, but that was practically suicidal.

"I see." There was a pause, and then he asked, "What is it that you think I can help you with?"

"I would like to know exactly what was said on that plane that night. I know it's been a decade, but you overheard their conversation. I hoped you might help."

Lance held his breath. Palance didn't have to do anything for him. From what he had heard, he had retired over five years ago. Word was that he had a heart attack. The last thing he probably wanted to do was talk to the son of someone blamed for killing one of his colleagues.

He hated that he was relying on his pity.

"Let me see what I can do. I'll call you in a few days."

Lance's face split into a grin. "Thank you, sir. I really appreciate..."

The line had gone dead. Not one for social niceties, it seemed.

After staring at the ended call notification for a moment, he slid his phone back into his pocket. He hadn't heard back from the other two calls he'd made earlier, one to the old investigator, and one to Joe's jump partner. After the note showed up in his Jeep, he'd decided he couldn't delay making inquiries. Even if the note wasn't related, if Joe or Mitch found out about it, it would set off alarms and draw attention he didn't need.

Back inside, he settled in his bed, folding his arms behind his head and closing his eyes. It was a start. He would begin with the pilot, and then work through the rest of the witnesses. There had to be more here. Why would his father, a seasoned veteran, jump the wrong way? Especially when the spotter had told him not to. He'd done hundreds of jumps. Why was this one different?

Maybe one of them made a mistake, but not three jumpers. Something was missing. He was going to find out.

Meg's face flitted behind his eyelids. He squeezed them tighter, turning onto his side and jabbing the pillow under his head. What had happened, at Stack Park…she wasn't ready. Not to hear him out, and not to learn about all of this.

It was best if he kept her at arm's length.

Chapter 8

The next three days passed in a blur of PT and exhaustion. In that time, he had to tolerate a few more missing items. His sunglasses, some socks. He started keeping the bulk of his stuff in his Jeep or at his grandmother's.

Apparently, that encouraged whoever was messing with him to leave a dead snake in his pack.

Maybe he should consider himself lucky. It could have been a live snake.

The only times Lance saw Meg was during training. She didn't stay in the bunkhouse with the jumpers, and that was probably for the best. The less he knew—about her, her whereabouts—the better.

He was proud of himself. He played it cool, the epitome of professional. It didn't keep him from watching her every chance he got, especially when he was sure no one else was looking or at least when everyone else was looking, too. While she led their calisthenics, for example, he thought all sorts of things. Things she'd dislike him thinking.

Unprofessional things.

He couldn't control his thoughts, though, could he? At least nothing he'd tried had worked. It was tough to pretend his grandmother was leading training when Meg and her toned body were there on full display for him. Hell, yesterday had gotten warm and she'd stripped down to only her tank top and sports bra. If the damn sexy play of her muscles as she ran in front of them didn't jack up his libido, the fine trail of sweat at the small of her back definitely did. Her skin glowed when she was hot, and he wanted to put his hands all over her.

As a distraction, he poured himself into training. He pushed hard, doing his best to sweat out his constant thoughts of her. Though it might work to some degree when he was awake, he couldn't escape dreams of her at night. Maybe it was exhaustion, but he'd wake up, hard and wanting her. If the physical stress of training didn't kill him, this might.

She was really something. All day, he appreciated her strength as she led them through endless runs and calisthenics. She did as many as they did. If she wanted to pass through jumper training, he had no doubt that she could.

Which made him wonder why she wasn't here, alongside him and Hunter and the rest of them. If it ever came up again in conversation...

Who was he kidding? The last thing he should do is try to talk to her more about personal stuff, like he shouldn't want to know where she was all the time. Because the more he knew, the more he wanted to know. He needed to keep focused on finding out about their fathers off the clock, and on the clock, he needed to keep his nose down and focus on work.

The trainers—Mitch, Meg, and the two jump specialists—knew exactly how to push them to the peak of their potential and yet keep them out of the hospital. When he was sure he couldn't give anymore, one of them or one of the seasoned smokejumpers would mention that he could quit, that they'd help him pack, and he'd shut up and push a little further.

They did endless calisthenics, two daily runs, and pack hikes. In the plus column, their packs were usually lighter. The last hike, he only had to fill it until it weighed ninety pounds. Con? The trails weren't flat. At the end of the day, he'd fall into bed, a heap of aching muscles.

Kevin washed out. There was no fanfare when he left. At the end of the second day, his room was cleared out.

That left the six of them, vying for four slots.

He hadn't done much to befriend any of the other guys. Digger and Rock seemed nice enough, and under other, less competitive circumstances, they might have been friends. Digger didn't say much, and Rock said too much, but both were decent enough guys.

Something about Sledge, though, rubbed Lance the wrong way. He was too...perfect. Everything Lance wasn't. While Lance set his sights on final outcomes, looking for every way to reach the desired result, Sledge followed every rule, focused entirely on the minutiae.

As far as Lance could tell, the physicality of this phase would prepare them for the intensity of detailed and job-specific training to come. While Sledge focused on the intricacies of each task, Lance settled for pushing himself to the limit. It might be ugly, but he went all out. The better prepared he was physically, the easier the rest of this would go. The two of them had taken the first and second spots in the class—Sledge for his attention to the intricacies, Lance for his balls-to-the-wall approach.

As a result, Sledge had set his sights on Lance as his main competition. It started with remarks about his performance under the guise of helpfulness. Suggestions for how he should sort the contents of his pack, for easier lifting. Lance mostly gritted his teeth and stayed quiet through all of that.

On the fifth day, they learned the fundamentals of a proper exit from an airplane door. Then, they were introduced to the exit tower.

The exit tower looked like a cell tower, but at the top, a fake airplane door was rigged to a zip line. They would hoof it up the flights of stairs in full gear, and practice their exits. They learned about the proper form, how to tuck their knees, how to fall. The rest of the crew's procedures. They'd jump and then ride the sturdy cable to the ground, unclasp, and run back up the stairs. It was the closest they could get to simulating a real jump without being in the plane.

Of course, Sledge offered Lance pointers. Again, Lance tried to ignore the guy. He had no desire for full-scale war with one of the other rookies.

There were limits to his tolerance, though.

At the end of the session, as they stripped out of the custom-made yellow jumpsuits that all smokejumpers wore, Sledge couldn't seem to stop running his mouth. "If you keep your knees in, Roberts, I bet it would help," he offered, his voice deceptively innocent in a way that made Lance's jaw clench. "You'd think, with your father, that you'd know better."

Lance's fingers halted on the zipper of his suit. "What would I know, Hammer?"

When he found out the guy's full nickname was Sledgehammer, he'd immediately nicknamed him Hammer in his head. Because the guy was as subtle as a hammer.

Sledge's smile sharpened. "That careless mistakes can get people killed."

Lance stepped up, right into the guy's face. This had gone on long enough. He didn't want a fight, but he wasn't going to back down from one if it was brought to him. "If you have something to say, just say it. All this pussyfooting around is for pussies."

"Fine." Sledge dropped his gear on the ground, his chin jutting out. "I think you're a risk. You push when you should be cautious. You aren't careful enough. In fact, you're borderline reckless. Word around the Redmond hotshots is that it runs in your family." He crossed his arms over his chest. "You should know I'm watching you."

Though Lance didn't look away, he could feel that the others had gone silent.

So...this happened faster than he'd expected. He assumed that the other rookies would hear about his father. He'd only hoped it would take a few more days, maybe into next week, after they'd had more time to formulate their own opinions about him.

What pissed him off the most was that Sledge's words weren't entirely false. Sure, he could be reckless. Caution wasn't exactly his default setting. He focused on getting the job done, not about making it pretty. And fine, he took risks, but only if the benefits outweighed the costs.

That should mean something, shouldn't it? After all, he worked his ass off and he wasn't sloppy, not when it mattered.

This was a blatant play to discredit him with the rest of the rookies.

"You're full of it, Hammer," he gritted out. "I'm not afraid of you."

"You should be." Sledge grunted. "I don't know how you got in here, but this whole place stinks of playing favorites. There's no room for that in a job this serious and I'm going to make it my personal mission to make sure that you aren't a danger to me or anyone else."

"Playing favorites?" Lance laughed. "If you think I got in here because of favoritism, you're crazy." If he'd heard the story of his father, he knew that was ridiculous.

"Maybe. Maybe not." Sledge shrugged. "Between you and the Buchanans"—he snorted, casting a glance at Hunter—"it's legacy stink all over."

Hunter stiffened, his mouth tightening.

The injustice of it squeezed Lance's chest, made him clench his fists. "Leave Hunter out of it. He's got as much right to be here as any of us. Everyone knows Joe Buchanan only picks the best. His reputation is beyond reproach. Anyone who says otherwise will answer to me."

"Right. Joe Buchanan, Will Buchanan. Hunt here." Sledge nudged his head toward him. "Even their sister." The side of his mouth tilted up. "I mean, she's fine to look at and all, but I'm sure I'm not the only one who wonders what she had to do to get that cushy job."

Lance moved before he thought. He ducked his shoulder into Sledge's gut, and the two of them hit the ground. The force of it was satisfying. He caught a lucky jab to the guy's kidney before he was yanked off of him.

Two sets of strong hands held him up, and two shoulders dug into his chest. It was only when the blood stopped pounding in his ears that he heard Hunter's voice. "Cool it, you idiot. You're playing into his hands."

Logic crushed him along with the realization that he might have just thrown away all of his dreams of ever being on this or any other smokejumper crew.

What the hell had he done? Of course, Sledge was baiting him. Hearing him talk about Meg had made him lose it. But he'd never have let anyone talk about Meg like that when they were younger and he sure as hell would have none of it now.

"Roberts. Buchanan. Nunez. My office. Now." Mitch's face was a mask of fury.

But it was Meg, standing next to him, that struck him in the gut. She looked as if she'd stepped into a schoolyard brawl too late.

He didn't know how much she'd seen or heard, but less was more probably.

This was it, then. Mitch spun, stalking toward the air center. Dak's mouth was tight and Hunter's face was unreadable. They'd been the ones to stop him, then. Not fast enough, but that wasn't their fault. He slapped them each on the shoulder, thanking them silently.

Well, if this was it, then so be it.

A few yards away, he caught Sledge's smirking grin. And, because he never left well enough alone, he gave the douche-canoe the finger.

That done, he didn't wait for a response. He followed the head trainer inside.

* * * *

Mitch's door hadn't been closed in months. Maybe years. The jamb stuck when he tried to shut it. When he moved it earlier, for privacy during his questioning of Sledge and Hunter, dust had erupted into the air.

Lance sat outside that closed door, waiting.

Sledge had disappeared inside first. Lance couldn't hear what was said, but he could imagine it.

Something like: Lance came at him first. And Sledge was only joking. Maybe a little bit of, should someone with Lance's hot temper and unstable personality be able to work on a team of smokejumpers?

Lance gritted his teeth, thinking about it.

It probably got worse. Sledge, the victim. Lance, the bad guy.

To some extent, he got it. He shouldn't have gone after him. He wasn't a teenager. He didn't get into those kinds of stupid fights anymore. At least he didn't think he did. When he was younger, sure. He'd been rowdy, unfiltered. Young and stupid, flipping his shit on the regular. Here? There was too much on the line to put himself in jeopardy this way.

Surely, he wasn't still that guy, that impulsive and hotheaded. He shifted, the possibility making him squirm.

Except...he couldn't stand what Sledge said about Meg. It was foolish, but hearing those words fall from his mouth, words that denigrated her...

it made him sick and mad in a way he'd never felt before. The only thing he had been able to focus on was shutting him up, making him pay for daring to talk about her like that.

He had to admit: that was pretty impulsive.

Sitting here for the past twenty minutes as first Sledge, then Hunter talked with Mitch, he recognized that Sledge had planned that. If Rock could see that there was some history between him and Meg, then Sledge could, too. The guy was a dickhead, but wasn't blind. Even though Lance had been on his best behavior since he'd talked to Meg, he was sure he still watched her a little too much for a little too long. His eyes followed her when they shouldn't.

Not much he could do about that.

It gave Sledge ammunition, though. And he'd used it.

The door in front of him opened and Hunter stepped out. He didn't look at him as he walked by, leaving the door open.

"Come in, Lance." Mitch motioned from his desk.

Lance stood, wiping his sweaty palms on his pants. He hated how nervous he was. It would be a whole lot easier if he didn't care if he got thrown out of here. But he did.

He stepped inside, remaining standing in front of his desk. He could feel Meg behind him, against the wall, but he didn't look at her. He had no idea how much she knew. Sledge hadn't offered his nastiness about her, he was sure of it. Whether Hunter did or not was a crapshoot.

Worse, Lance had no idea what was acceptable to say. He decided to let Mitch take the lead.

"Seems you had a busy day, son." Mitch leaned back in his chair, studying him.

"I suppose so, sir."

They gazed at each other. Lance didn't look away. He wasn't ashamed of what he did. If someone else defamed Meg right now, he'd do the same thing again, in a heartbeat. If he was going to get thrown out because he stuck up for one of the most decent people he knew, so be it. He needed to look at himself in the mirror tomorrow.

"I'm letting you stay," Mitch proclaimed abruptly.

Lance exhaled a breath he wasn't aware he was holding. "I'm staying." He repeated the words as if he needed clarification. Maybe he did.

"Yes." Mitch lifted his eyebrow. "This is your warning, though. I won't tolerate fighting in my crew. If you ever pull a stunt like that again, if you're a distraction in any way, you're out. I don't care what the reason is." He glanced past Lance to where Meg was standing behind him.

As Lance couldn't see her, he couldn't decipher that look. She might not have heard all of the gory details, but she'd gotten enough. He nodded. "Thank you, sir. I won't let you down."

The supervisor nodded back.

Lance didn't linger. Turning, he caught Meg's gaze. Looking away, he hightailed it out of there. The ramifications of Mitch giving him a pass—how Mitch must feel about it, how this would look to the rest of the team, what they would assume when Lance stayed after going after a teammate—he didn't know. More, Meg wouldn't appreciate that he connected them so personally. Not at all.

He had to keep his head down and do his job or he'd never find out what happened with his father.

Outside Mitch's office, he rubbed the back of his neck. Even as he decided again to keep it cool, he wasn't the sort to turn away if he felt someone needed him to step up. Especially Meg.

He only hoped that wouldn't be the case again.

Chapter 9

It took Meg a full day to catch Lance alone. The task was made more difficult because she didn't want to look like she was trying to get him alone. But, the night after Lance took Sledge to the ground, she found him in the loft, packing a chute bag.

Now in the second week, the trainees had spent the better part of the past two days learning about smokejumper gear. As their field was so specialized, they needed to custom make the majority of the things they wore to do their jobs. That included their jumpsuits—made out of specialized, fire-retardant fabric and boasting pockets all over to carry gear—and their parachutes.

Each recruit was required to learn to repair the parachutes and stuff them into their bags the right way. There was a rigorous set of checks and balances to ensure that every chute was safe and ready for activity at any time. The rookies would pack and repack chutes so many times over the next few weeks, they'd be able to do it by muscle memory, or that was the plan.

Most of the time, the jumpers who needed time alone could be found up here in the loft of the bunkhouse, repairing gear and packing chutes. The constant togetherness of the air center could weigh on them, she guessed. For the most part, the jumpers thrived in the wilderness. Being cooped up inside with so much company made them all a little stir crazy. They'd come up here to do this ever-present and monotonous work and find some peace and quiet. A couple of them were even pretty cocky about their skills with a sewing machine.

That's where she found Lance on Sunday night. The recruits had been given a few hours to leave, get some food, blow off some steam. She heard

Rock and Digger ask Dak to go into town to have a beer. She assumed Lance had gone with them. Apparently not.

"Hey," she offered. He glanced up, then back at the pack he was working on. Not encouraging. When he continued his work, his brow still tight, she tried again. "Mind if I join you for a minute?"

"Sure." He grunted, yanking on the pack. "But, probably not best if you're trying to avoid me. Remember? We need to stay professional."

She debated running. She could leave, walk back downstairs. Go back to her mom's place. She bet her mother hadn't made anything for dinner. Over the past week, her mother's floundering mental state had become clearer. She went to work, but nowhere else. After work, she came home, got into her pajamas and sank into the couch. Sometimes she even slept there, only waking for her next shift. If the boys didn't have to get up to go to school, Meg didn't doubt her mother would stay on the couch and sleep forever.

She could go home, feed her mother, try to pull some words out of her.

Or, if she wanted the easy route, she could drive back to Bend. See her friends. Shawn, the guy she'd been casually dating, called her earlier in the week, asked if she was busy this weekend. Going to Bend, though…nothing about it appealed to her. There was so much going on in Redmond. She was ashamed to admit she hadn't thought of Shawn at all while she'd been here, and she hadn't returned the call. She could text him, if she wanted.

Instead, she stepped into the loft. She probably could have texted Lance. She'd even debated it. But, there were things she needed to say, and she wanted to say them to his face. Texts wouldn't do the trick.

Might as well get it done. Besides, the longer she put this off, the more awkward it would be. She didn't want weirdness between them, had been trying to make it better, not worse.

Meandering forward, she attempted to defuse the tension. "Stuffing chutes?"

He nodded. As she gathered her courage, tried to decide how to begin, she watched him carefully fold, then refold the material until it met his satisfaction. Again, as it had repeatedly over the past week, his attention to detail and his intense drive to master everything they did here struck her. Today alone she'd mentioned to Mitch that Rock might not be taking the minutiae of tending to smokejumper gear seriously enough. While she liked him, she feared that he didn't have the focused determination the job required. This was serious work, and he might not be able to do what needed to be done.

Lance could. She'd watched him prove it again and again.

He gathered another chute and started the ritual to pack it. She lifted one of the parachutes he'd already packed, studying it. She'd sat in on the training session. Without a word, she checked all of the points. "This looks great."

"Yeah." He placed his hands on top of the bag he was working on. Tilting his head, he met her gaze. "What's up, Meg?"

His features were guarded, as if he wasn't sure if he should ask. Or, as if he wasn't sure he wanted an answer.

"I wanted to thank you." She trailed her fingertips along the table they used to pack chutes, tracing the dents and imperfections in the finish. This table had been here for years, decades even. So much history. "For coming to my defense with Sledge."

He nodded, returning his gaze to the pack. "He was an asshole."

"Yes. But you didn't have to say anything to him." He still didn't meet her eyes.

"Hunter was there," she reminded him.

Sledge and Hunter had told wildly different stories. Sledge insisted Lance jumped him when he denigrated his job performance. He'd gone on about how someone so hotheaded was a risk to their group, how he had reservations about working with him. Mitch had listened, his face unreadable. Meg had stewed.

When Hunter came in, Mitch asked him the same simple question, "What happened?"

Her brother's face twisted and he stared out the window over Mitch's head. The pause went on long enough that she wondered if he was even going to answer. If it had been Joe, Hunt might have exploded, but he didn't know Mitch, and he didn't want to make a bad impression.

Finally, he said, "Sledge said something awful about Meg."

His eyes found hers, his brows lowering. Maybe he disliked Lance, but he wasn't going to let that stop him from defending her.

From there, the whole sordid story came out.

Wasn't it exactly what she'd worried about? Not so much this, maybe. She'd expected the recruits to speculate that she was given the job based on her family's name. She hadn't expected that anyone would assume she'd slept her way into it.

Sledge might not even believe that. From both Hunter and Lance's reactions, he might have only wanted to see what they would do, if they'd blow their tops. As far as tests went, it was a good one.

She might not agree with it, but she understood. Still didn't like the guy, but she got it.

"You don't have to thank me." Lance tugged on one of the straps. "You went to bat for me. Got Mitch to let me stay. I should be thanking you."

"I didn't, actually. I didn't have to." She shrugged one shoulder, tapping her finger on the table. "Hunter did."

That stopped him, his hands stilling on the pack. "Hunter?"

"Yeah. I didn't hear what Sledge said, so he filled it in. Then he said that you were protecting me, and said Sledge was out of line."

There was a pause. Then he said, "You've got the whole picture, then." He pushed away, turning to stack the three parachutes he'd bagged, pulling another to work on.

"I don't think I do." She'd seen her brother's face. Hunter had been a split second from jumping Sledge. Lance had beaten him to it.

He grunted, noncommittal. Nope, that wasn't going to work. She needed answers. "Why?"

"Why what?"

"Why'd you go after him? Hunter was there."

"I'm faster than Hunter. Always was." He still didn't look at her.

She didn't buy that. "You know what I mean. Why did you do that for me? Hunter would've handled it. Maybe not how you did, but he would have gotten the message across. Why did you go after him, Lance?"

He leaned forward on his hands, his gray eyes meeting hers. "I wouldn't have let anyone talk about you like that before. That hasn't changed."

It was a vow, and she didn't doubt it. She smiled softly, leaning against her hand on the table. "Just like another brother."

She'd meant the words to break the tension. She could barely breathe through the strained conversation. He was agitated, like he was frustrated with her. It had to stop. Her job, his job...their careers depended on them being able to work together, without all this pent-up tension.

If he saw her as a sister, someone to protect, someone to tease, but not as anything more serious, it was probably better that way, from a professional standpoint. At least then, they could be friends, go back to their old comfortable relationship and leave this horrible animosity behind.

Even if they could never be more, she could use a friend.

She missed him.

Except he didn't smile back, didn't laugh it off, like she hoped. His gaze darted away to focus on the table in front of him as his head dropped between his shoulders.

"I'm not your brother," he gritted out, his hands gripping the edge of the table.

She blinked, stung. "I know that."

"Then don't say it." He pushed back and away from the table. He retreated two steps back, putting space between them. As if she was dangerous.

"What do you want from me, Lance?" Exhaustion crushed her. It had been a long week. She'd hoped they could figure this out, but they seemed to speak different languages these days. Maybe she should just go. "I wanted to thank you for sticking up for me. I did. I'll leave you to whatever you're doing."

As she turned, determined to leave with as much dignity as she could manage, his voice stopped her. "You don't get it."

"No. I don't." She spun to find his face a mask of frustration. "When we were younger, I tagged after you and Hunter. You had to know I had a huge crush, but you never made me feel stupid. Even that one time…" She didn't want to revisit the day she'd leaned in, her eyes closed. Her lips had probably been puckered, like some cartoon character. "Back then I knew exactly where I stood. I watched you date pretty, popular girls, and I settled for being your best friend's kid sister. I thought we were friends. At least I hoped we were." She lifted her hands in exasperation. "Now, though, I don't know what the hell to think. You almost got thrown out of jump training defending me. And…"

She paused, inhaling a shaky breath. She should stop here, before she made an even bigger fool of herself. But, she'd come this far. Might as well go all in.

She met his unreadable gaze. "I thought you were going to kiss me. At my mom's house." There. The words were out. "Now you don't even want to talk to me. So, yeah. I don't get it at all."

She blew out a shaky breath. The exhale didn't make her feel any better. Saying all those words hadn't fixed anything either. The closed look on his face? Definitely not helping.

She should have left while she was ahead.

He moved so fast, it stole her breath. Three long strides brought him to stand in front of her, only a breath of space between them. He lifted his hands, as if he was going to reach for her, maybe cup her face, but hastily he ran them over his hair before dropping them to his sides.

"God, Meg." His voice was low and gravely, and the scratchiness of it sent a shiver along her spine. "You…" His gray eyes held hers, searching, pleading. "I never saw you as just Hunter's little sister. That was always the problem."

Her heart fluttered, the racing of it so strong she shook with it, with the need to step closer, to fall against him. His scent, a mixture of the wind and spicy soap, along with something raw and warm…she breathed in. She might never get enough of that smell.

"I was supposed to. I never could quite manage it." His whispered words fanned her face. "And to be clear…I wanted to kiss you at your mom's house. I still want to kiss you now."

The words, smooth as honey, as softly spoken as a lullaby, broke over her skin. She licked her lips, her gaze dropping to his mouth. He'd been going to kiss her? Did he really still want to kiss her?

"Please. Stop." At his pained words, her eyes met his again. His jaw was tight, and his hands clenched and unclenched at his sides. "Stop looking at me like that. I already want to touch you so badly it hurts."

The air between them heated. She could see it play out. She could tell him that she wanted that too, that she couldn't remember a time when she didn't want to kiss him.

If he'd touched her, she would have done it. She didn't think she was strong enough to withstand the intensity of his gaze and his touch at the same time. Kissing Lance Roberts would fulfill ever girlish dream she'd had and, if she was honest, a few of her full-grown woman dreams, too.

"But this…it doesn't change anything." He stepped back two steps. He shook his head, his voice just above a whisper. "There can't ever be anything here, between us."

The words slammed into her with the force of a wrecking ball. As he turned away, returning to the table, she rubbed her forehead with her fingers. "You said…"

He tilted his head up to the ceiling, and when he spun back, he chuckled. "I know what I said. But you're still my trainer. And I'm still a recruit. Starting anything with you…not a smart idea." He shrugged. "Besides, even if you weren't in charge of my training, you said you don't get involved with firefighters. And I'm definitely a firefighter. That isn't going to change."

Searching his face, she tried to find any trace of the heat she'd seen there before.

She hadn't imagined it. And she hated how much she'd liked being something he wanted. It was as if someone had dangled candy in front of a child, promising to share, and then changed their mind at the last moment.

And of course, he was right. The space between them allowed the years of insecurity to meld with all the concerns of today.

His arguments were sensible, responsible. They were the exact reasons she should have offered to stay away. Hearing him voice them…brutal.

She had some pride, though. So, she bit her lip and squared her shoulders. "Of course, you're right. I agree completely." She glanced at the parachutes, anything to stop looking at him.

"Why don't I look these over, to make sure they're good. As your trainer."

"You don't have to—"

"No." She managed a smile, but it was painful. "I don't mind at all." Nothing was going to make her run away.

He shrugged, shoving a bag toward her. "I've packed these three."

She scanned the pack, went through the usual checklist. His eyes burned through her the entire time, and though she didn't want to squirm, didn't want to run, there was only so much she could take.

Finally, when she'd looked over all of them, she pushed back. She was leaving a piece of herself there, on the table in the loft. "Looks good. I'll leave you to it."

* * * *

As she walked backwards, away from him, he forced his features into a grin that would probably condemn him to hell. It hurt his face. He tucked his hands into the pockets of his Carhart pants, so he could hold them still, keep from reaching for her.

"Thanks. I appreciate it." He couldn't believe how breezy the words sounded.

"Right. Of course."

"Meg..." Her name was a groan on his lips.

"No." She closed her eyes, and when she opened them, she'd put her shields up. "Seriously. You're right." Her mouth twisted in what he assumed was her attempt at a smile. It sliced his stomach into ribbons.

"Always." The word came out by rote.

"I mean...about us."

He could not listen to this. Having a front row seat while she mentally agreed with why he was a bad idea...already awful. Hearing her voice the words? No thanks.

He'd been truthful. Taking a chance on them was risky as hell. It affected her job. It would cause a rift in her family. Hell, he was a wild card. He had been gone for ten years. She didn't know him anymore.

Even if they could work through those obstacles, he was still a firefighter—a smokejumper—like her brothers, and like their fathers before them. And none of that compared to what he might find if he kept digging into their fathers' deaths.

It would be better—personally and professionally—if this didn't even get off the ground.

He tried a smile. He'd been faking this kind of smile for a long time and he hoped it was convincing. Returning to the table, he put some much-needed space between them. "Absolutely. This—" he waved his hand between them, in the space he'd created. "This is a no-go."

"Right." She nodded again. "You're not good for me."

The words were knives. "Exactly. No worries, firecracker. We're good here. I swear." He nudged his head at her. "See you around."

He needed her to go, before he said something he'd regret.

Not that he would take back anything he'd told her. Nope. In fact, admitting that he'd spent forever wanting her...God, that part had been liberating. He didn't keep secrets well, lived in the moment. Holding back didn't suit him at all.

It hurt to look at her, to keep the stupid grin on his face. When she finally nodded and waved before backing down the stairs, he exhaled a shaky breath, leaning forward on the table and letting his head fall between his shoulder blades.

It was for the best. Every rational part of him knew that to be true.

He only wished it was different.

When he came home, how had he believed he could fix everything? He snorted, shaking his head. Maybe he'd be able to fix some things, but this? This wasn't one of them.

He needed to leave her alone, learn to pretend she wasn't there, that he didn't want her every second of every day.

Except...he wasn't that good of an actor.

Chapter 10

Monday morning, Lance stood at attention alongside the remaining recruits.

It had been a long night. After Meg left him in the loft, he'd been unable to focus. He'd gone to bed and been unable to sleep.

In front of him, Will and two other seasoned smokejumpers stood next to the packed chutes the recruits had been working on all weekend. Each of them had been tasked with packing the chutes, putting their initials on them. Last night, in need of a distraction, he'd gone over the three he'd packed over and over, checking and rechecking the straps and the folds. He'd done it perfectly, like Meg said.

The three smokejumpers went through each pack, picking them apart and praising or criticizing the recruits' techniques.

Lance did his best to concentrate on Will and the others, but when Meg stepped out of the air center with Mitch, his focus shifted to her, as always.

God, she was gorgeous. Her auburn hair caught the morning light, and her flawless pale skin looked translucent. But it was her mouth, those full, rosy lips. He ached all night, thinking about them. When he'd told her he wanted to kiss her, he'd watched her mouth slip open, her tongue touch her bottom lip, and he'd gone so hard he'd wanted to groan with it.

"Who the hell did this?" Tim, one of the older jumpers, lifted a chute. The material had gaping slashes in it, as if someone had taken a knife to the fabric.

Will inspected the pack on the ground, the bag Tim had obviously pulled the chute out of. "It's got Roberts's initials on it."

"Roberts." Tim's shrewd gaze found him. "What do you know about this?"

"Nothing, sir." He couldn't look away from the mangled equipment. The chutes they used were expensive. Because their job was so specialized, they custom made a lot of their equipment, including their parachutes. This was a costly act of vandalism.

And a chute he'd packed.

He forced himself to hold Tim's eyes, even though he wanted to look at the others, search for guilt. Did someone else in the rookie class want to see him fail so badly that they'd destroy smokejumper property to get it done?

"You didn't notice this chute was ripped when you packed it?" Tim's eyebrows lifted.

"The chute wasn't ripped when I packed it." It was the truth. He'd checked every parachute for the smallest imperfections. "They were perfect."

Whoever sabotaged that chute was sending a message, the same message he'd gotten in the note in his Jeep, the same message he got every time something of his was taken or ruined. They wanted Lance gone.

Who the hell was it? Sledge, in retaliation for jumping him the other day? Guy was a giant dickhead. Still, Sledge was a rule follower. Even Lance could tell that his biggest issue with him was that he wasn't. Lance made him nervous.

He definitely didn't seem the sort to destroy smokejumper property.

Who then?

Whoever it was, they were becoming more daring. He could write off broken things or a note as a prank. This was something else.

Lance needed to watch his back.

Had someone learned he was looking into his father's death? Had that pissed someone off enough to wreck smokejumper property?

Tim's face tightened. Lance could see the rash of shit he was going to get for this. Hell, if he'd willfully packed the chute, he'd deserve it. But, this wasn't his fault. Even while he braced himself for whatever chewing out he was about to receive, he seethed.

He would have never done that.

Meg's voice sliced through the air. "I checked his packs."

Tim spun to study her. His face smoothed, the way a lot of the smokejumpers seemed to when they dealt with her. It was a mixture of politeness and a little wariness. She hadn't earned her place here yet. "You did?"

"I did." She wrapped her arms around the clipboard in her hands. "I checked out the loft last night, while Mr. Roberts was packing his chutes. I thought he might appreciate another eye—I'd sat through the training as well, wanted to see how I'd do." She added an open grin then. "I looked them over. They were done correctly."

Her fingers trailed along the decimated fabric in Tim's hand. "Someone must have done this after he left." She dropped her hand, her mouth tight, and her eyes met his.

Their conversation last night stretched between them. The weight of it tightened his throat. Even after he had hurt her, purposely put distance between them, she stuck up for him.

The trainer glanced at the parachute. Lance watched unease pass over his features. A smokejumper's equipment was an extension of them. This was a gross violation. His outrage was understandable.

He watched realization dawn. None of the recruits would ruin the equipment, not like this. They might make mistakes with it or miss something out of negligence. This went beyond negligence to malevolent.

Someone had tried to set Lance up. To scare him. Maybe to scare them all.

This went past trying to get Lance thrown out, though. Someone had slashed at the fabric with a knife. Hacked it up.

This threatened violence.

Tim nodded to Meg before addressing Lance. "Roberts. Is that true?"

"Sir, I swear to you that I would never knowingly ruin smokejumper materials." He hoped the other man could hear his conviction, and if he caught a little defensiveness, so be it. Hell, he was pissed off. He'd spent his entire adult life trying to prove that he wasn't the kind of person to cause a scandal.

That he wasn't his father.

"I saw his packs last night," Meg repeated. "I'm certain if you give him the chance, he'll be able to replicate them."

Tim glanced between them, and then nodded. He tossed the tattered parachute on the ground, disgusted. "This is unacceptable. I don't know who did this." He stared at each of the recruits, his eyes as sharp as daggers. "If I find out, not only will you be removed from training, I'll call the cops."

"Sir," Lance said. "I'll repair the chute." He hadn't made the mess, but the offer might go a long way toward repairing trust. The last thing he needed was any of the trainers deciding he wasn't worth the effort. Stunts like this were a distraction.

Damn it. One more thing to worry about here.

"Fine." Tim's face tightened. "Let's go for a run. If someone here has the time and energy left at the end of the day to wreck our equipment, then maybe we aren't working you guys hard enough."

Lance mentally groaned. He understood the point of this, showing the entire group that the actions of one affected them all. But, he couldn't help wondering if it wouldn't also breed animosity toward him.

"Be dressed in five."

As they all trotted off to the bunkhouse to prepare, Lance caught sight of Meg.

She'd defended him. By doing so, she'd outed them, that they'd spoken last night. That she was speaking to him privately. He couldn't imagine that was a good thing for her job. Even if she'd only been checking on his work, it still suggested preferential treatment.

Why had she gone out on a limb for him? He appreciated it, but it had probably been damaging for her. She should have stayed out of it, for her own good. He could have handled it himself.

Even as he thought it, he acknowledged that it was easier this way. She had more credibility than he did. And, though he hated that she'd had to do it, he couldn't help but admire her guts.

God, this woman. Every time he had himself under control, she did something else to make him want her even more. Not just because she was gorgeous, though that didn't hurt. But because she was so incredibly unselfish, such a fine person.

He tore his gaze from her.

The guys were going to go out for a drink tonight. Their first practice jump was tomorrow, and everyone was a little nervous.

Maybe he should tag along. It would be better than spending another night alone in his room, hard and wanting her.

* * * *

The music in the lounge in Bend was louder than Meg remembered. She didn't listen to club music regularly, but she'd never noticed how hard it was to think with it on.

Her two girlfriends, Charlotte and Olivia, sat across from her at the high-top table. Olivia was a nurse in the practice where Meg worked, and Charlie was a physical therapist they used. She'd begun her practice in Bend only a couple years ago, but Meg liked working with her. She was incredibly thorough and universally admired by her clients.

Charlie sipped from a cosmopolitan and asked, "So, are they all good looking?" She had to yell over the music. Her eyes crinkled at the corners, her expression teasing.

Meg had been fielding questions about the smokejumper recruits since she met the girls tonight. She took a sip of her red wine and forced a smile as she yelled back, "They're in top physical shape. That's my job."

"Yeah, but are they hot?"

She rolled her eyes, trying to deflect.

Olivia clapped her hands together, squealing. "Can we meet them?"

Meg laughed with her friends, but it felt wrong. Probably because it was fake. She didn't see them like that. The recruits at the air center were in great physical conditioning, and they'd only gotten more toned in the past nearly two weeks. But, thinking of them like that negated the sense of purpose in what they all did there. It reduced hours of work, of expertise, of intense seriousness, to girlish fantasy.

Fine, they were hot. They were physically attractive, sure, but that wasn't the half of it. There was something so sexy about someone who was doing a job that not that many people would or could do. It overshadowed how they looked. While they were enough to send the libidos of women far and wide into spasms, the smokejumpers and rookies at the base were also professionals who took their jobs of saving lives very seriously. Pretending they were just a bunch of pretty faces made her uncomfortable. She respected them, every smokejumper and smokejumper recruit she'd worked with so far. Their professionalism, their dedication. Pretending that she didn't opened an unwelcome chasm between her and her friends.

For the past two years, she'd hung out with these women. They'd shared drinks, gone to dinner. As they socialized, she believed she was building a life here in Bend.

Now, she wondered if that life was actually as satisfying as she'd once thought or if she had been fooling herself.

Her eyes shifted to the others in the club. She'd run here, to Bend, after college, because she needed a job. At least that's what she told herself. But, maybe she'd run from her family in Redmond, from all the ways they'd weighed on her. Had she realized her mother was faltering in Redmond? Yeah. Not to the extent she'd found recently, for sure. Back then, she believed if she left, maybe her mother would take some initiative to take control of her life and stop relying on Meg to do it for her.

Propping her chin in her hand, she wondered if that was true, or if she'd left Redmond because it was easier. She'd become a physician's assistant because, like the rest of the Buchanans, she wanted to help people.

But working here was easy. Anyone with her degree could do her job. The smokejumpers...every time they went up in that plane, they risked themselves for others. They saved both property and lives. Working with them was more rewarding than anything else she'd ever done.

Sitting in this hip bar populated with other young health professionals, she could see her life play out. Find and marry one of the well-dressed men in her field, someone else who helped people. Maybe even someone who came here. Keep working for Dr. Colman. Have children.

It was a solid plan. It was a lot like many other women's plans. She should be happy with it. It could be enough.

Except… those years in front of her, they were dull, completely boring. Would she always wonder what would have happened if she'd chosen a different path? A path more like her brothers?

She was doing meaningful work. Helping others, being a physician's assistant, it was important. She saved lives, if not directly, she sent people to specialists who could save them. It might not be as flashy as the work her brothers and Lance did, but it was good work. Important work.

Glancing at her drink, she smirked. Who was she kidding? There was no comparison. Her life in Bend didn't fill the void.

She belonged in Redmond.

What had happened? A month ago, she'd been happy. Or she'd believed she was happy. Then, Lance came back into her life and suddenly nothing felt as shiny. Was it him? Was he the reason for this sudden dissatisfaction with her job, with her life?

He'd stood in front of her yesterday and lied to her.

There was something between them. She could feel it and he admitted it. He'd said there couldn't be anything between them, but he didn't get it; there was already something there. Even thinking of him now, a shiver coursed along her spine. With his gray eyes and his intense gaze, the way his stare seemed to look inside her…she'd chalked her memories of Lance up to a teenage crush. Except it wasn't only girlish emotion. She witnessed how hard he worked, and she watched firsthand how considerate he was. The way he listened so intently, hearing her meaning and not only her words.

As an adult, she recognized how important and rare that was, and it made him even sexier to her. This man…he was more than the boy he'd been—better—and she found him irresistible.

She might pretend she could find that connection anywhere, that one of the men in this bar would give that to her, but she knew better. She never felt the same for another man.

Unfairly, her thoughts strayed to Shawn, the doctor she had been seeing. He was nice enough. In fact, he was a catch. Lots of other girls in the hospital would kill to date him. But he paled in comparison to Lance.

Everyone did.

He was hiding something. Whatever it was, it had been enough for him to push her away. Her mind strayed to the slashed chute. What was going on?

She didn't know the answer to that. But she was going to find out.

The bar's walls felt too close around her. It was time to leave.

She swiped her phone from the table and dropped it in her bag. Reaching in, she snagged her wallet and retrieved the two twenties she'd slipped there earlier. Dropping them on the table, she pushed back and stood up.

"Where are you going?" Charlie asked, setting her martini on the table. A pang of guilt seized her gut. She'd been the one to organize tonight's get-together. Leaving early was poor form.

"Sorry girls," Meg said. "I'm tired, and I have an early day tomorrow. I should really get going." She pulled her cardigan off the back of her chair and draped it over her arm.

"But we were going to get dessert." Confusion clouded Charlie's face. Meg never skipped dessert, said it was the one benefit of running as much as she did. She never had to pass on sweets.

"I left a little extra. Dessert's on me." She gave a little wave. "I'll see you guys soon. Maybe a movie next week?"

Olivia wiggled her fingers at her. "Sounds good. And I want to hear more about sexy jumper bods. You can't keep that stuff to yourself."

Meg laughed. "I'll come with lots of details. Promise."

As she slipped out of the bar, she noticed a few appreciative glances, even from some handsome, well-dressed guys. None of those men did anything for her. The only one she could think of had expressive gray eyes and a need to jump out of a plane to fight wildfires.

A glance at her phone said it was nearly midnight. She couldn't see Lance tonight. He had his first jump in the morning and she'd been drinking. She wasn't leaving Bend. But, tomorrow, after his training jump, they would talk. She was going to get answers.

Getting involved with Lance would be complicated. Professionally, this was a horrible idea. But it wasn't only that she was his trainer. It was her family, it was their history, and it was his future as a smokejumper… all of it. The whole package was dangerous.

Even as she debated, she worried there wasn't anything left to debate. It was like they were two trains on the same track, heading toward one another. It felt inevitable that they would crash.

And just as unavoidable.

Outside, keys in hand, she walked the two blocks to her downtown apartment. She slipped in, but was struck by the stark reality that there was nothing here for her.

If her desire to prove she was tough enough to be a smokejumper had driven her to Redmond, the purpose and fulfillment she'd found as a trainer at the air center was what would keep her there. Besides, her mom, the twins? They needed her.

For once, that didn't feel like such a heavy weight.

Chapter 11

The morning of Lance's first jump dawned sunny and cold.

As the new recruits gathered their things and packed their gear into the many pockets of their jumpsuits, the tension was thick in the air.

They'd spent hours, days, preparing for this jump. They'd gone over the logistics of exiting the plane, they'd packed and unpacked dozens of parachutes. They practiced call signs and instructions...they were ready.

This wasn't the first time Lance had jumped out of a plane. He'd gone sky diving lots of times. He loved all of it. Base jumping, bungee jumping, skydiving...it all fed his need for adrenaline. The rush. On land, there were only so many ways to get that feeling. He loved to ski and surf, but nothing beat the pure thrill of falling through the air, heading for the ground faster than a speeding car.

As he fastened the last buckles on his suit, he caught a glimpse of Rock standing next to him. His skin was a little green. The last thing he wanted was the guy to puke on him when they were at fifteen thousand feet. "You okay?"

"Sure. Never better." Beads of sweat trickled along his temple.

"It's going to be fine. Standard jump. Nothing fancy, right onto flat ground." As far as Lance could tell, it didn't get much more straightforward than this.

"Only jumped a couple times. Not afraid of heights, but that's a small plane." Rock glanced out at the airstrip then checked the cage on his helmet. His hand shook slightly.

Lance slapped him on the shoulder. "No problem, man. We got this."

"You sure, Roberts? Trouble seems to follow you around." Sledge's voice cut into their conversation, smooth and full of derision. "Don't want anything to happen to you."

"Appreciate your concern, but you should watch yourself." Lance didn't bother to give him a glance. The guy didn't deserve his full attention. If anyone should get kicked out for being a dick, it was that guy. "No one likes you."

Sledge laughed. "Yeah, but they trust me to do the job. Can you say the same?"

He smirked before sauntering away.

"All right, rookies," yelled Tim, as he finished fastening buckles on his jumpsuit. "You all went through your initial sign offs?" A chorus of affirmatives answered. He nodded. "Good. Then grab your sacks, and let's get on the plane."

As they all shuffled out, the engine of their plane hummed in front of them. The smell of airplane fuel permeated the air, and together the smell and the sound filled Lance with anticipation.

He was really doing this. Finally, after years of preparation, after all the hours of training and sweat and tears, he was finally going to take his first jump as a Redmond smokejumper.

Adrenaline coursed through him as he climbed in behind Hunter and took his seat next to him. They still didn't talk, but the ice between them had thawed. After he'd defended Meg to Sledge, Hunt had changed. Not welcoming, but not quite as frosty either. They coexisted. It was better than before, so he'd take it.

As the plane taxied down the runway and they ascended to their altitude, no one spoke. Around him, the faces of the men he'd been training with for the past two weeks were identical masks of determination and intensity. He'd only known them for a brief time, but he was already coming to rely on their talent and expertise. Even Sledge, who he didn't trust personally, showed real talent and skill at everything he did. Even so, he was happy he wasn't that guy's jump partner. He and Hunter had been paired this time.

Finally, after what felt like forever, Tim stood and moved to the front of the cabin. "All right rookies. Time to show us what you got. Let's do this."

He went through the final jump instructions and after a few minutes, he nodded to the first pair, and they strapped in.

They lined up, all of them in their full-face caged helmets and high-collared jumpsuits. Rock and Sledge went first, waiting for the taps from Tim, the spotter, before jumping out of the plane at a tuck. Finally, Hunter stepped into the open door. From behind him, Lance felt the lick of the wind, could feel it pulling at him, beckoning him out into the open air, like an old friend welcoming him home. He was eager to greet it, too.

Hunter received his smack and launched into the sky. With the opening empty, Lance stepped forward, dropping into the sitting position.

Except, below him, Hunter's chute didn't open.

"Reserve, Hunter," Tim said, his voice sharp, as he hit Lance on the shoulder and he jumped.

The moment of exhilaration sang through his blood, the same as it always did. These periods of wild insanity, the seconds when he was completely at the mercy of the elements...they were the moments he was most alive. The freedom coursed through his veins and he laughed.

Only then did he see Hunter below him, his parachute still twisting in a tail behind him.

Why hadn't he cut the parachute, deployed his spare?

The starkness of the situation crushed the euphoria from his jump. If their primary parachute malfunctioned, they were trained to get rid of it, so they could dispatch their spare chute. For some reason, Hunter wasn't able to get rid of his.

He didn't have a working parachute. Below Lance, he continued to speed toward the ground.

Reaching into his side pocket, Lance pulled his knife and quickly cut the cords of his parachute. Immediately he dropped like a stone, his stomach raced into his throat. Craning his neck, he searched for his old best friend, sighting him to the east 300 yards below him and dropping fast.

Hunt had always been smart, though, and he made his body big, the friction of his suit and his outstretched limbs slowing him the best he could. With the tangled parachute dragging him down, he spun in the air and Lance could tell he was having difficulty keeping himself angled toward the ground. Tucking his hands at his side and drawing his legs together, Lance dove forward, streaking through the air, racing to Hunter's side. He prayed his aim was right, and that he didn't overshoot. He got lucky. As he closed in, he gripped the knife that would save both of their lives. With his other hand, he grabbed Hunter's right arm and sawed at his tangled parachute line.

When the first line gave, any drag that Hunter had from the failing chute went with it, and the two of them together accelerated toward the ground. The sudden movement sent them spinning, and Lance struggled to regain his grip on Hunter's suit, straining to get at the remaining parachute line. Hunter wrapped his arms around his waist, doing his best to steady them. Reaching, the knife outstretched, and Lance made contact. One strike, another...with a final jerk the line shredded, and the parachute fell off behind them.

Hunter let go, and Lance pushed with his legs, diving away from his friend. Nearly simultaneously, their reserve packs discharged, sending their parachutes into the sky. But even as he felt the familiar tug of the chute, Lance knew they were too close to the ground.

They were moving too fast and there wasn't enough time to slow down.

They were also off target, by at least a mile, with no time to adjust. This was going to hurt like hell.

Desperately, he tried to remember all of the ways he'd learned to minimize a faulty impact. As the ground sped toward him, he tucked his knees and angled himself like he'd learned in training so that he could take his fall more to the side, potentially preventing any broken bones.

As he made initial impact, he wondered if a landing could hurt this much without breaking something. His back hit the ground and the air forced out of him, leaving only pain in its wake. He rolled to the side, gagging.

Waves of nausea hit him, and he swallowed again and again, doing his best not to vomit. Pain streaked along his spine, like a fire in his veins. Coughing, he looked around, trying to see where Hunter had landed. Out of the corner of his eye, he caught sight of a parachute, tangled in a tree.

He stumbled to his feet, ignoring the burning and aching. Though he couldn't feel parts of his body and the ones he could feel screamed in agony, he staggered toward his jump partner.

"Hunter! Hunter, are you okay?" The words were screechy, and he wasn't even sure if they were the right words. As long as he was making noise, Hunter would hear him. No response, though. He did his best to pick up the pace, but it was slow going. His ankle was sprained. It didn't matter now, though. He needed to get to Hunter.

As he closed in, though, all he could see was the dangling legs of his old friend.

He wasn't moving.

* * * *

"Tim said someone damaged the chute." Will crossed his arms over his chest, his feet shoulder distance apart. Like he expected a fight.

"What do you mean?" Meg asked, pacing the length of the hospital waiting room. "Someone packed it incorrectly?"

"No. We checked all the equipment. No evidence of tampering after inspections. Somehow, though, someone got to the parachute." Will's lips pursed. "They twisted it."

"Someone sabotaged it." The buzzing in her ears was louder than what was coming from the overhead fluorescent light. "Someone tried to hurt him." Hunter could have been killed. He could have tumbled to the ground.

Falling like a stone.

Will shook his head. "No. We're trained to lose a tangled parachute. We all wear backup canopies. He would have cut it and deployed his other backup. Hunter lost his knife. Probably nervous." He pulled his arms tighter against him, staring out at the top of the next building. "Lance managed to get to him, somehow, and cut the cords himself."

"This is...horrifying." Meg paced across the waiting room in the hospital, her hands on her hips. Down the hall, Hunter was still in surgery. "Someone planned to...scare Hunter? Make him use his backup?" When Will didn't respond, she swallowed around the dryness in her throat. "Or someone was trying kill him."

Will exhaled sharply. "Let's not overreact."

"Why would anyone do that?"

"I don't know."

She pressed her palm to her forehead. "Lance. He could have been hurt, too. What the hell is going on?"

"Who's to say this wasn't his fault?"

"Please, Will. He saved Hunter. We're lucky he was there today."

"I think you've got a soft spot where he's concerned. I don't think you see him like the rest of us do." Will's jaw tightened. "And now this happens. Bad things follow that family around."

"You aren't giving him a chance." She sighed. Will rolled his eyes. He wasn't going to listen to her. Not tonight. Not with Hunter in the surgery room down the hall. She would have to talk to Joe about this when she got back. She changed the subject. "How is Hunter?"

Will exhaled. "The doctor says he has a long road to recovery. They're going to replace his rotator cuff, and his leg is broken. He's definitely out this year, and next year is in jeopardy as well."

"He's lucky he got out with his life." Meg shook her head. This was exactly what she worried about all the time. Hunter and Lance hadn't even been fighting an active fire. They could've been killed on a routine training exercise. It would keep her up at night.

It always kept her up at night.

Will must have read her mind. "It was a fluke. Hunter lost his knife, or it would have been fine."

Her anger spiked. Who did he think he was talking to? "Please. After what happened to our father? You can't talk to me about flukes."

He stared at her, probably because she brought up their father. She snorted. He had no defense. It was his job, like it had been their father's job. If he defended himself, he made himself a target with her. He didn't want to do that, not tonight. Not with Hunter in such bad shape. Instead, he asked, "Did you call Mom?"

"Yeah. She's on her way." Her mother's voice on the phone had been all wrong. She hadn't cried, she hadn't yelled. She'd accepted the news with an icy calm that settled deep in Meg's heart. It was as if, after father died, her mother was always bracing for the worst. And she never stopped.

Will buried his hands in his hair, tugging softly. "This wasn't supposed to happen."

"It's never supposed to happen. But, it does. In our community, it does."

"Come on, Meg. There are lots of other jobs that are dangerous, jobs that need to be done. Jobs that save lives."

"Does that mean I have to be happy that my family does those jobs?" Her brother lay in a cold, hospital surgical room. And Lance...they thought he'd sprained his ankle, and he was covered in bruises she heard. If he had hit a tree like Hunter, he could be the one on the operating table.

She didn't want to think about that either.

The door to the waiting room opened, and Hunter's doctor, Dr. Banks, stepped inside, his face mask hanging around his neck and his sleeves rolled up as if he'd just finished scrubbing. "Meg. He's all done."

"How is he?"

"He came through fine. He's young and healthy." Dr. Banks lifted his hands. "That's not to say he doesn't have a long road ahead, but he'll get there. And if he's anything like you, he'll do it in record time."

She sighed, the relief making her dizzy. "Thank God."

"When can we break him out of here?" Will asked.

"He's got to suffer through our hospitality for at least two more days. We have to make sure the new joint I put in his shoulder takes, and we need to be certain he's clear of infections. He'll spend tonight in the ICU, and tomorrow we'll move him to a regular room."

Meg nodded, holding out her hand to the doctor. "Thank you. I appreciate all your hard work." Banks had an amazing reputation. He'd been at a charity dinner tonight and had come in specifically to help her brother because her boss, Dr. Colman, asked him to. She appreciated it. Bend was larger than Redmond, but the health care community was relatively small. They took care of their own.

"No problem. Happy to help." He shook Will's hand, gave them a few more details and instructions, and left.

In the now-empty waiting room, she and her brother couldn't seem to find words to fill the silence. All they had been doing lately was arguing. When had they come to this point? She mourned their old easiness. Finally, she pointed to the door. "Why don't you head home? I can wait for Mom. I'll stay here tonight, in Bend, at my place." She could use a night away from her mother's place. Solitude.

"Are you sure? I can stay, you know—"

"I know. It's no big deal." She tried for a smile. "This is my regular stomping ground, remember?"

He grinned back, but it looked as forced as hers felt. "If you say so." He stepped forward, folding her into his arms.

It had been so long since one of her brothers had given her a hug—a real hug—that she stood stiffly in his embrace, before folding her arms around his waist and tucking her head against his chest. She breathed in his familiar smell, closing her eyes, and wishing things were different between them. Everything was so hard. She wished she could span the divide, but she didn't have a path forward with him. She wasn't sure she ever would.

"Night, sis. Try to get some sleep, okay?"

She nodded and waved as he left her alone in the waiting room with the silence. The television was on, tuned to a cable news show. The banner streamed across the bottom of the screen, but she didn't read any of the words.

How was Lance? Had anyone come to visit him? His grandmother didn't drive anymore, and she didn't know who else he had in the area to look after him. Had Dak come? She hoped so. If anyone deserved someone to care for him, it was Lance.

She wanted to be at his side at times like this.

She shouldn't. It was a recipe for heartache. He'd warned her away. It spelled professional disaster. She didn't seem to care. Right now, all she could think about was whether he was comfortable, if he was okay. It wouldn't change whether she was with him officially or not.

Before she changed her mind, she set off for the nurses' station. She recognized one of the nurses. "Hey, Annabelle. How are you?"

"Hi, I'm good. I heard your brother was here. How is he?"

"In recovery. Stable, right now. Thank you for asking." She smiled. "I was wondering, though, if you could look something up for me."

She leaned forward on her elbows. "Sure. What do you need?"

"Can you tell me which room Lance Roberts is in?" She shouldn't be looking him up, not here. It was overstepping ethical bounds. Right now, she didn't care.

Annabelle entered a few things into the keyboard, and her brow dropped. "You said Lance Roberts? I'm not finding anyone by that name."

"Are you sure?" Surely, they hadn't discharged him so quickly?

"Wait. Here. Says he checked himself out earlier." She leaned back, away from the computer.

Meg patted her palm against the counter, glancing down the hallway. He checked himself out? They would've wanted to run lots of tests, check for internal bleeding. At least. There's no way he would've gone through all of that testing in that amount of time. "Okay. Thanks a lot for checking."

The other girl nodded as she answered an incoming call.

Meg pushed away from the desk, retrieving her cell from her bag. Pulling up her contacts, she started a message to Lance.

Hope you're okay. She fired the text off quickly. Pausing, she warred with herself over whether she should say more. She shouldn't. But that didn't stop her from going on

I'll be at my place in Bend. If you need me. She hit send, and then she added the address, before she could overthink it.

She slipped her phone back into her handbag and set off for the waiting room. She was being ridiculous. He wasn't going to call her. He wasn't willing to take a chance on her.

Hopefully, though, he was with someone who was taking care of him.

Her phone rang, and her pulse picked up. But it was her mother.

She swiped to answer the call, and propped the phone up to her ear. "Hey Mom, where are you?"

Chapter 12

Lance killed the engine, resting his palms against the steering wheel. The apartment building in front of him looked like every other apartment building in small, urban towns. Cookie-cutter windows, low-maintenance brick facade...there was no way to tell which unit Meg lived in. The place had no personality, no distinguishing character.

It was the opposite of where he expected Meg to live.

What was he doing here? He should go back to the bunkhouse, get a good night's sleep, and prepare himself for the judgmental stares of the other recruits and jumpers tomorrow. But her text...

Was she okay?

He left the hospital as fast as he could. Couldn't stomach the places. They wanted to run a bunch of tests. MRI, CT scan. No way. He was fine. And if he wasn't, Joe Buchanan would have another excuse to fire him. He wasn't going to let that happen. Better that he not find out.

So he hightailed it out of there, before they found anything to keep him. Before he left, though, he asked about Hunter. It took some convincing, but he got the nurse at his station to spill that he was still on the operating table. A little eavesdropping and he learned that they were working on his shoulder and his leg was broken.

Fuck. This wasn't how it was supposed to go.

He closed his eyes. He ran through the events after their plane exit. He'd seen Hunter's parachute tangle, he tried to think of all of the ways he could have done things differently, all of the ways he could have kept Hunter out of the hospital.

But he couldn't find anything he would've done differently. He slammed his palm against the steering wheel. Not Hunter...

He tried to imagine how his old friend must be feeling. They had always dreamed of becoming smokejumpers. An injury like this, it could sideline him for a year, longer maybe. Even forever. If there were lingering issues, he might never fight a fire again. Someone like Hunter, he didn't deserve this.

And Meg...she was going to take this hard.

He should leave. He needed to be her friend, to keep his cool around her. Showing up at her place at 9 o'clock at night, it was too intense for friendship. He should send her a text. Ask about Hunter, see how she was doing.

But even though it would be smarter to do that, he had to see her, to verify with his own eyes that she was okay.

He was only going to stay for a minute. Someone was probably there. Meg had so many friends, a huge loving family...she wouldn't need to be alone, not if she didn't want to. He was just going to go up, make sure she was fine, and then he was going back to the air center, where he belonged.

Decided, he plucked the keys out of the ignition, and threw open the door. Stepping out, he winced as he put too much weight on his sore left foot. He had no idea how he was going to run on that tomorrow. But that was a problem for the morning.

Limping through the door of the nondescript building, he made his way past a bank of mailboxes on his right. Scanning the names, he found her. M. Buchanan, apartment 211. Tapping the sticker with her name on it, he headed for the elevators.

The whole ride up, he debated whether or not he was crazy. Probably. But he wouldn't be able to sleep. He might as well check on her, since he was already here.

The elevator dinged. Stepping out, he followed the arrow toward her apartment. At number two hundred eleven, he inhaled a deep breath, listening for voices inside. There was only silence. He knocked three times.

The sound of a deadbolt unlatching greeted him, the knob turned, and the door swung open.

Meg's face was free of makeup, her gorgeous auburn hair pulled back into a low ponytail. In low-slung sweats and a camisole, she was more coed than successful physician's assistant and trainer of macho firefighters.

And she was the sexiest thing he'd ever seen.

He tucked his hands in his pockets to keep from reaching for her. "Hey."

It wasn't much by way of snappy greetings, but all of his intellectual conversation had flown out of his mind at the sight of her.

"Hey." Her hand rested on the door jamb. She'd kicked her hip out to the side, and the angle gave him a view of bare skin over the waistband of her sweats. "You came."

"You texted." It wasn't much of an explanation. In fact, he probably should have texted back. That would've been the proper thing to do. But it was all the reason he had.

"I did," she said, swinging the door open. "Do you want to come in?"

There was nothing he wanted more in the world. But he shrugged. "I came to make sure you were okay."

"Don't you think I should be asking you that? You're the one who fell out of a plane today." Meg inhaled a broken breath, and caught her lower lip between her teeth, but not before he noticed its quiver.

"It's okay, firecracker. I'm fine." His voice was gruffer than he'd like, but watching her worry was ripping him apart. "A little banged up, that's all." Look at him. King of understatement. He had more stitches than he could count, and a bum foot. But, he hated how concerned she was.

Because she was one of his trainers. That was all. Not the one to complain to.

Yeah, and he was in denial.

She studied him, and he couldn't help but think she could see right through him. "I bet. You checked yourself out of the hospital. Why didn't you stay, finish your tests?"

He shrugged. "Feel fine. Don't need any more tests."

"You could have bleeding…"

"Meg, I'm fine." He chuckled, rubbing his head sheepishly. "How's Hunter?"

She sighed. "In a lot of pain. Still processing. They haven't explained the full extent of his injuries to him yet, but I don't think he is ready to deal with exactly what's in store for him." Sadness weighed on her features. "Hunter doesn't get a cold well. He's going to hate everything about rehabilitation."

Lance grimaced. He could relate. He was a caretaker…his mom, his Gram. He hated having people take care of him and being laid up in a treatment facility would suck. "How long is he in the hospital?"

"Few more days. Then they'll move him to the rehab center. Who knows how long he'll be there?" She glanced over his shoulder.

Time for him to get to the point. "Listen, Meg…I came to tell you…I've gone over it a dozen times. More than that, probably. And I can't think of any way I could have saved him."

It was the truth. He didn't know if she would believe him, didn't know if anyone would believe him, but it was the best he had.

Her clear blue eyes met his, full of sorrow. "Is that what you think? That I blame you?"

"God, I don't know. If you did, you wouldn't be the only one." He rubbed the back of his neck. "I'm already beating the hell out of myself. You can jump on that bandwagon."

"Someone messed with the parachute." Her mouth thinned. "Will told me."

"Good lord." He buried his hands in his hair. Hunter had picked up his parachute. Not one he packed, the one he was supposed to jump with. That parachute had been meant for him.

He turned away from her, staring at the fluorescent lighting above him.

It should have been him. The guilt crushed him so thoroughly, it squeezed the air from his lungs.

"You saved him." She stretched the words out, as if he wouldn't understand them if she spoke them quickly. "You helped him get his reserve chute, you saved his life."

He wasn't ready to take that, but God help him, he couldn't exactly tell her that though he might have saved him, he wouldn't have been hurt if it hadn't been for him in the first place.

Instead, he snorted, finally mastering his face enough to turn back to her. "His leg is broken and he's sporting some new hardware in his shoulder. Some saving." His words sounded bitter, even to his ears.

She shook her head. "You don't see yourself right. That's not what I heard happened." She paused. "You're a hero, Lance. You risked yourself to help him. You might not like that, and that might not be how you see yourself, but I do. Nothing you say is going to change that."

Looking into her eyes was like looking into the sun. So bright. They awakened hope in him that he had no right to feel. When he looked at her, he could almost believe her. God, he wanted to. Through her eyes, he looked different. Not the cause of someone's pain. Whole, worthy.

This had been a bad idea. He shouldn't have come. This visit...it was only going to make it harder for him to keep any distance. It would leave him wanting more, when he had no right to do that. Not while he was investigating their fathers.

Not when it should have been him.

"I should go. I only wanted to check on you." He was repeating himself. He stepped back, away from her, away from everything he wanted.

"No." The one word had the strength of a cymbal crash. She squared her shoulders, and she stepped toward him.

His heart kicked up as she lifted her hands, cupping his face. He had been waiting so long for her touch. Closing his eyes, he tried to inhale, but his chest felt too tight. Her soft hands...it took everything in him to remain still, not to move, not to reach for her, too.

"Lance." Her voice was a siren call. He steeled himself, determined to hold it together. But when he opened his eyes to meet hers, it was his undoing. She smiled up at him. "Come inside."

Everything inside him tore apart.

"God, Meg…I can't, not unless you want me to touch you." Her eyes widened, her mouth opening, and she leaned forward, relaxing into him. He shook his head, backing away so that her hands fell from his face. "You don't understand. You don't want that. When I made you that promise, it was as much for you as for me. Our jobs, our families…and there are things here, things you don't know…"

"So tell me."

"I can't." He didn't recognize his voice. It was too raw, full of longing. "I want you and I want to tell you. But, I can't."

She followed him, into the hall, and placed her hand on his chest, right over his heart. The heat from her touch, it burned into his soul. "I don't care. All I know is that today, you almost died. You saved my brother's life. And I…" Her eyes were soft, so soft. "Come in. Hold me. Please."

He reached for her like a starving man offered his last meal. His arms curved around her slim back, and he pulled her against him with reverence.

He shouldn't. God, he should leave now. But, he couldn't.

As he dropped his head and covered her mouth with his, he didn't think he'd ever tasted anything as sweet as the soft gasp she made.

Chapter 13

Meg's kiss, the taste of her mouth, it was better than he'd imagined. With a low growl, he deepened the contact.

He'd been waiting to kiss her forever. Not only the past week since their near miss at her mom's house, but since they were kids. He couldn't remember a time when he hadn't wanted her. Not just physically, but he'd ached for the right to hold her, to kiss her, for the moments when she'd want him to do that, when she'd allow him that privilege.

He was going to make the most of it.

Favoring his ankle and leaning on the wall to support them, he backed them into her apartment without breaking the contact of their mouths, closing the door softly behind him. He pulled away briefly to fasten the deadbolt, but he returned as fast as he could, his mouth against hers again.

He didn't want to spend longer than he needed to away from her.

Pressing her into the wall in her foyer, he ran his hands along her face, down her shoulders, along her sides. Every inch of her was so incredibly soft. She panted, and her head tilted back, giving him delicious access to the bare expanse of her neck and collarbone. He could kiss her mouth forever, but the temptation to taste that warm, creamy skin...it was too much.

Dragging his mouth from hers, he trailed his tongue along her jaw and down her neck.

Her pulse beat quickly there, and he pressed a soft kiss to it before moving on.

She strained against him, her fingers pressing into his shoulders. Spanning his fingers, he pulled her closer to him, bringing her entire length against him. If she didn't know how much he wanted her before, she definitely did now.

"We need a bed," he murmured against her throat, forcing himself to lean back, away from her, even while his entire body screamed for more.

Grabbing his hand, she led him toward the bedroom. Her grip was tight, as if she didn't want to break the contact between them either.

In her bedroom, her reading light was on and she left it. An open novel lay face up on the bed, clueing him in to what she had been doing before he got there. She picked it up, and dropped it on the side table. The low light cast a soft glow over her skin.

He closed the gap between their bodies. Smoothing his hands along her back and up to her shoulders, he pulled her against him, taking her mouth again. He went slowly, determined to take his time with her. He'd already waited a lifetime for this, he could definitely make it worth the wait.

Her bare skin was silky under his fingertips. He needed more of it. Tucking his thumb under the straps of her camisole, he pulled them down over her shoulders, placing kisses as he went.

"Meg?" he whispered, sliding his fingers under the top of the camisole. "Can I ditch this?"

"Absolutely."

He didn't need more encouragement. With a soft tug, he pulled the tank top down. She wasn't wearing a bra. He covered her small, rose-tipped breasts with his palms and swallowed her gasp with his kiss.

God, everything about this, touching her, holding her, it was exactly what he'd always wanted. Not because he'd been saving himself for her these years, because he hadn't. He'd dated other women. Sometimes he'd go out with the same woman a few times, sometimes a couple months. No matter how long, no matter how hot the sex, the relationship would cool. It wasn't conscious. He would find that he didn't seek out their conversation or he wouldn't actively want to see them, to hear what they had to say. When he noticed, he would end it because he wasn't trying to be a dick. He just didn't see the sense in letting things go on if his heart wasn't in it.

But this? Everything about holding Meg touched him somewhere else. This woman had grown up with him. She'd cared about him when no one else saw him. She'd run with three boys and had held her own. She was strong, loyal, and fierce.

And now, she would be his.

Dropping his head, he took the tip of one breast into his mouth, sucking gently. Her fingers smoothed against his shoulders, pulling him toward her. He gathered her closer in response, nearly bending her backward.

Her lithe body bore all the signs of regular runs and hard work. She was long, muscled, and gorgeous.

He backed them up, and they tumbled together onto the bed behind them. Her hands found the bottom of his shirt, tugging it up his back and over his head. He ducked out of it, flinging it on the floor and returning his mouth to hers.

Her hands had gone to the waistband of her pants. Lifting her hips, she shimmied them over her backside and slipped them down her legs and over her bare feet, leaving her only in a modest pair of white cotton bikini panties.

She followed his glance, shrugging. "I wasn't expecting company."

He chuckled as he tugged at the button on his pants and pulled his fly down, wiggling out of his jeans and tossing them on the floor with her clothes.

He gathered her in his arms, him with only his boxers on, her in her cotton panties. As all their bare skin connected, they both stilled. Her eyes found his, and she looked concerned. He ran his hand over her cheek, smoothing his thumb over her forehead. Maybe he was attempting to rub out the wrinkle he found there. "Hey. You okay?"

She shook her head, but her concern remained.

He pressed again. As much as he craved going further, as much as he wanted to keep running his hands along the rest of her body, he mostly wanted to make sure she was happy. "We can stop. You're not ready for this. We'll stop."

She gripped his biceps, her hold firm. "No, that's not it at all. I don't want to stop." She swallowed. "I want to be with you. I've always wanted to be with you."

It seemed like their entire lives had been leading up to this moment, as if he'd been waiting for her, for this. Maybe there were things that should hold them apart, but right now, whatever was happening between them was inevitable.

He leaned toward her, kissing her softly. From there, though, the chemistry between them became undeniable. He didn't want to go slow, his need for her pushing him forward. She didn't mind, though, matching him for intensity. He covered her face, her shoulders, and her breasts with kisses, reveling in the taste of her on his tongue and his lips.

He tugged her panties down, his hands shaking. When she was naked beneath him, he inhaled sharply. "My God. You're gorgeous."

When she might have blushed at another time, now her eyes only shined up at him, full of tenderness and something intense that touched him somewhere he hadn't known needed to be reached. She pulled him toward her, giving him a kiss that broke him open.

He needed to taste her.

He trailed his mouth down her body, across her stomach, until he settled between her legs. Pressing her thighs open with his palms, he ducked down, and placed his lips to the soft folds.

This was definitely the sweetest part of her.

He groaned, and then ran his tongue along the tender flesh, and she rewarded him with a soft cry, her fingers flexing into the blankets. He forced himself to focus through the buzzing in his head. Watching every flex of her muscle, every gasp, he began the gift of learning what she liked, what made her shiver and gasp.

He settled in, determined to make her come, but when he thought she was getting close, she shimmied up. "No."

He leaned up on his elbows, his stomach dropping. "No?" She wanted to stop? Now? That was not what he'd expected to hear.

She laughed. "Not no, stop. No, I want you to be inside me."

He grinned, her confidence making him tighten further. He shimmied off the bed, dropped his boxers, and reached into his pants pocket for his wallet, retrieving the condom he had there. Rolling it on, he returned to the bed, leaning on one knee, before he caught her looking at him.

She had her bottom lip tucked between her teeth and was staring at his dick. The admiration there made him groan. "Meg, stop."

She laughed again, shifting to the side and patting the bed. "Here."

He cocked his head, questioning.

"Lie down," she said.

He did as she asked, and she straddled him. The muscles on her strong legs flexed, and he ran his hands along them, helping her position herself above him. In the dim light, her skin was rosy, flushed. She stared down at him, and as she placed her hands on his lower stomach, the muscles there flexed.

That was nothing compared to how it felt when she began to lower herself, taking him inside her.

His head kicked back, and his eyes closed as he groaned with the feel of it all. Her inner thighs flexed against his hips, and she used her hands against his stomach to help her balance as she lifted and lowered on him.

He forced his eyes open, needing to watch her. Her eyes were closed, and her head tilted back. The position jutted her breasts out, and her nipples were tight and deep rose. The lines of her belly and the curve of her hips… she rode him slower than he'd like, as his body roared for release, but he didn't hurry her pace. He wanted to savor this, the vision of her.

Though he was beneath her, he didn't mind not being in charge right now. He spanned his hands across her hips, dipping his fingers into where they were joined to softly rub her clit, and she jerked, her inner muscles squeezing him in response and causing him to groan again. He kept up the soft pressure with his hands as she leaned further back and into his fingers. Her eyes lifted, still heavy-lidded, and the desire there dried his mouth, made him determined to do whatever it took to bring her pleasure, give her whatever she needed.

When her pace increased, he rocked slightly to meet her, and she came. As she gripped him, both inside and out, he fell apart beneath her, holding her hips and their connection as she fell forward, her breasts against his chest.

As their breath returned to normal, he pulled her closer, believing that the weight of her against him was the most delicious mass of all.

If he'd believed that he was making her his, he had been fooling himself. Being with Meg touched him in ways he'd never expected, ways he'd never known he needed. He would never be able to pretend they didn't exist again.

He was hers.

* * * *

Meg woke slowly, her head tucked under Lance's arm and her hand curled on his chest. She was warm, both because she was snuggled up on him, but also because the air conditioning didn't work well in her little apartment.

She didn't move as her eyes flickered open.

They'd slept together.

She always suspected that if they gave into the heat between them that she wouldn't be able to stop herself. When she sent the text to him earlier, she'd known that if he reached out, if he offered to kiss her again, she wouldn't stop him. She only hadn't expected things to progress so fast after that.

Maybe she should have. She'd wanted him her entire life. Their lovemaking had stirred emotions she'd never felt before. Though she didn't take sex lightly and she'd slept with other men she'd cared about, this had been a completely different animal.

It had all felt right.

Now, though, in the aftermath, all the reasons why she'd doubted in the first place came rushing back.

Tomorrow, they'd go back to their real lives, the same life that also included her brothers and mother who wouldn't accept their new…situation. She was still his trainer, at least for another two weeks. After that, how was she going to explain their new intimacy when she was an authority figure in the spring?

None of that was more complicated than his job. Caring for someone like him was playing with fire. And she did care for him, whether she wanted to or not.

"Whatever's going through your head, you should stop." His sleep-husky voice broke into her thoughts.

She grinned, her cheek moving against his chest. "I was just thinking about how this changes everything."

He rubbed her shoulder. "You should save thinking for later." As if to press home his point, he covered her mouth with his.

With his lips on hers, she ran her hands along his back muscles, pressing her fingertips into her shoulder blades. She leaned into him, allowing his smell, his taste fill her senses.

She dreamed of his kiss for years. It was as good as she imagined. Not soft, but not hard. Firm, without being overpowering.

Perfect.

Their mouths played against each other, fitting like a hand in a glove. Against his chest, her nipples tightened, and her heart pounded in her ears. With her eyes closed, she allowed him to overwhelm her senses, and the exhilaration of being so close to him blocked out everything but the two of them.

He tangled his hands in her hair, angling her mouth so he could take her lips more fully. She opened further for him, and when his tongue slipped against hers, she met him equally.

This is what she'd always wanted. Lance. Holding her, wanting her… the reality was better than her dreams.

Now that she'd allowed herself to touch him, she wasn't sure if she'd ever be able to stop.

When it was over, she lay in his arms. Into the silence, she said, "I didn't want to fall for you."

"I know."

"You're a firefighter. Like my brothers, my father. I already worry about them…" She pressed a kiss into his shoulder, beneath her cheek, and inhaled a shaking breath. "Now, I need to worry about you."

His chest rose and fell under her head. She beat of his heart under her hand was steady. He covered it with his own, squeezing. "I'll do my best not to make you worry."

He lifted her fingers, turning them to press a kiss to her palm.

She wanted to believe him, but she knew better. Caring for him carried risk. It was a recipe for worry and fear. Too late, though, to think about that.

She was already in love with him, had maybe been in love with him her entire life. Her only option now was to hold on the best she could and hope the fire didn't take him away from her.

Chapter 14

"The elevator is down the hall." The pretty receptionist pointed toward the east corridor, her dimple showing. "Want me to show you?"

"No, I'm good. Thank you," Lance said with a grin, rapping his knuckles on the desk. Sometimes being relatively good-looking came in handy.

He revisited everything he needed to say as he hurried into the elevator, and pressed the two. He didn't have much time because Mitch wanted them in the air center by 9:30. If he was late, so be it. Some things had to be said.

The elevator dinged, and he turned left toward Hunter's room. Around him, hospital staff bustled with early morning chores. The whole place smelled like institutional food and his stomach roiled. He'd picked up something for breakfast on his way. He refused to buy food here.

He paused outside room 227 and took a deep breath. Then, he tapped his knuckles on the doorjamb. "Knock, knock."

As he stepped inside, his first thought was that Hunter looked worse than he expected. His face was busted up, covered in stitches and black and blue marks. His leg was in traction, and his arm was covered in a wrap over his shoulder. He was pale. For someone in amazing shape, he looked as if the life had been stolen from him.

"Didn't expect to see you." The side of Hunter's mouth turned up in a pained grimace. "Then again, maybe I should have."

"How are you feeling?" As good a place as any to start.

"Like I have a broken leg and had to have shoulder surgery."

The comment was so typical of the old Hunter, it surprised a laugh out of him. As the familiarity faded, though, it was replaced by the new awkwardness between them.

Might as well get this over with.

"I want you to know I did everything I could…I mean, the jump… everything went bad." He shook his head. "I can't think of anything else that could've helped." When he practiced this in his head, it sounded a lot smoother. Didn't seem to be any good way to apologize for someone's injuries.

Hunter glared at him. "Wait, you're blaming yourself?" He chuckled, but it was wry, lacked humor. "Did you exit the plane badly? Are you the one that twisted my parachute? Because last I checked, that was all me."

"Hell, Hunter, you know everyone will think it's my fault anyway. I can't seem to do anything right." It was true, fair or not.

"Well that's bullshit. I was there. We're good here." Hunter glanced out the window.

Except they weren't, where they? "Listen, Hunter…I wanted to talk about something—"

"Are we really going to do this now? It's been ten years." Hunter twisted the sheet in his hand, his knuckles white. "You saved my life. I think we're even."

"It was never about even. And you know me well enough to know that I don't need any incentive to save someone." Lance exhaled his exasperated breath. "This has nothing to do with what happened yesterday. We used to be tight. And I screwed up. I should have come to see you after the fire."

Hunter sized him up. After a long moment, he nodded. "You're right. You should have."

So that's how it was going to be. Lance glared at him. "Yeah. I was an asshole."

"You're right. You were."

"And a bad friend."

"Yeah. That, too."

Lance rolled his eyes. "Anything else?"

Hunter stared at him. Lance refused to squirm. Either Hunt was ready to get over it, or he wasn't. He'd done all he could.

That didn't keep him from holding his breath.

Finally, Hunter grinned. It was a grin from the past, full of shared mischief-making. "Nah, that covers it."

That smile…it lifted a weight from Lance's chest, a heaviness he'd carried for years. Without it, he wanted to laugh.

"At least we got that out of the way." Shaking his head, he snorted. "Listen, I have to get back." He reached into the side table drawer, pulling out the standard-issue hospital and hotel room pad of paper and pen. He scribbled his cell phone number and tore off the top sheet. "Call me. Or text. Whatever."

He dropped the sheet of paper on the tray next to Hunter's bed, giving it a tap. Tucking his hands in his pockets, gave him a quick nod. "Later?"

"Yeah, man. Later."

They stood there grinning at each other for an extra moment. A quick rap on the door interrupted them.

"This a private party?" The door framed Meg, but it didn't do her justice. Lying next to her all night, he paused more than once to look at her. She was gorgeous, but he expected the shine of it to wear off. Yet here she was, as lovely as ever. More so. Because he knew exactly what she looked like, under all those clothes, and it was lovelier than he could've ever imagined.

That wasn't it, though. She was loyalty and protectiveness. She gave and gave, to everyone. To him, to her family. If she was only a sexy body, this might not be so dangerous.

But it was.

He cleared his throat, rubbing the back of his neck. "Hey. I stopped in to see your brother."

"I see that." Her smile grew. "Aren't you going to be late for work?" He wondered if she realized how much her teasing softened her face, made her completely irresistible.

"I was leaving now. Can I give you a ride?"

She nodded her head as she stepped in, squeezing his forearm. Awareness coursed through him. "No, that's okay." She smiled at her brother. "I'm going to hang out with Hunter for a little bit. Whether he likes it or not."

When Lance returned his gaze to Hunter, he realized his mistake. He'd completely forgotten that his friend was in the room.

How was that possible? When Meg was around, he couldn't think of anything else.

Until now, though, he hadn't realized how much of an issue that was going to be. The look on Hunter's face said he saw exactly what was going on.

How the hell was he going to keep their relationship a secret if his face gave him away every time?

Awkwardness settled in the room as Hunter glanced between them, back and forth. The smile smoothed off Meg's face. Apparently, she saw exactly what he did: her brother knew.

"I'd love some company," Hunter said, but no one believed him. His eyes settled on Lance. "You should go. Before you're late."

Meg's hand fell away, and she swept forward, to Hunter's side. With a little wave, she offered Lance a sickened grin. "See you later."

As he stared at the siblings, he took his cue. "Right. Later." Then he turned to Hunter. "Text me."

Hunter nodded, and Lance left before they could add to the weirdness.

In the hall, he wrestled with whether or not he should go back in there. What would he do, though? Have a conversation about how he'd slept with Hunter's sister? He just made up with the guy. Seemed cruel to start off with, "By the way, I've never had sex as amazing as what I had with your sister last night."

He wasn't ashamed. If anything, he didn't know how he was going to go back to the air center and pretend he didn't feel protective of her. Pretend she wasn't his. Even now, he wanted to go back inside that room, sweep her into his arms and kiss her senseless.

Probably wouldn't go over that well, though.

As he strolled out of the hospital, and into the parking lot, he exhaled. Meg said this wasn't going to be easy. He thought she meant because he was a firefighter, because her brothers hated him. Because she was his trainer.

He had no idea that it could be worse if her brother was a friend again.

If either of them found out he was looking into their father's deaths, he might lose them both again.

And this time would be much worse.

* * * *

"I thought you didn't want to play with fire." Hunter dropped his head back onto the pillow.

To avoid meeting his gaze, she stepped forward and pulled the pillow up, so he didn't get a crick in his neck. "I don't know what you're talking about."

He snorted. "Please. I'm your brother. I always knew when you were lying, I just didn't always tell Mom."

She chuckled. "Fine, then. How about it's none of your business?" She wasn't talking to him about this. What happened between her and Lance was still new. She wasn't ready to start hashing it out with Hunter.

Last night had been perfect. She had always known, or at least she had always suspected, that there was something between them. But the chemistry that had exploded last night had been volatile. It wasn't only that it was great sex, though that was part of it. What they'd done together… it had reached a spot inside of her much deeper, much more meaningful. There was no going back, not for her.

She didn't know what that meant. Was she trying to start a relationship with him? Because anything serious affected everything else in her life.

There wasn't much choice, though, not anymore. Because she couldn't imagine being without him again. There was no going back, but she didn't know the way forward.

"Maybe it isn't my business, but that doesn't mean I don't have anything to say."

"Of course," she said. "Because my love life requires your comment."

"This has nothing to do with your love life."

"It doesn't?" She glanced up at him, but where she expected judgment, all she found was concern.

"No, it has everything to do with Lance Roberts." Hunter shook his head. "I don't care who you fool around with, Meg." She offered a skeptical snort. Lifting his good hand, he smirked. "Okay, fine, maybe it bothers me a little bit that it's Lance. But that's not what I'm talking about."

"So what are you talking about?"

"There's something going on with him. And I don't mean just standard stress, or whatever else the other guys at training are dealing with." His mouth tightened. "Things around Lance are dangerous right now. Has he told you that his stuff keeps going missing?"

She shook her head. "What do you mean?"

"People are taking his stuff. And if they aren't taking it, they're ruining it. He had to start leaving his personal things in his Jeep, or at his grandmother's."

"How do you know? You've been ignoring him for the past three weeks."

"Just because I look like I'm ignoring him doesn't mean that I'm actually ignoring him." Hunter snorted. "I know what's going on around there."

Uneasiness settled in Meg's stomach. She didn't like to think that Lance was dealing with people trying to sabotage him. But she couldn't deny that Hunter was probably right. "The parachute…"

Hunter nodded. "Exactly. Someone did that. And he might want you to think that it was a one-time deal, but it isn't."

"What are you saying?"

Hunter blew out an exasperated breath. "Yesterday…my parachute. It was supposed to be his."

Heat flowed from the top of Meg's head down through her body in a slow trickle. "What?"

"It was supposed to be his. We traded, at the beginning of the day, I ended up picking his up as we were preparing, and he waved me off when I offered to hand it back. They're all supposed to be packed exactly the same way, so we didn't think anything of it. But now?" He exhaled. "The parachute was tangled. It shouldn't have been a big deal. If I hadn't lost my knife when we jumped, I would've cut the cord, and my other chute would have expelled appropriately. It would've been scary, but it wouldn't have been dangerous. At least not overtly."

"The parachute…it was supposed to be Lance's."

"Yes."

She shook her head. It didn't shake out the panic there, though. She shook it faster. No. That couldn't be. "Does…does he know?"

Even as she asked, it was clear. Of course, he knew. She told him that the parachute had been twisted. Lance was smart enough to put it all together.

"With his father's history…" Hunter's mouth firmed. "Some people don't want him around."

"Someone wants to kill him. And they almost got you killed." Anger coursed through her, and she could feel her face heat. "We need to tell Joe." This would require an investigation. Someone would pay for this.

"I was going to talk to Will first." He grimaced. "I wanted to see what he thought we should do."

"Well, now you won't know. Because I'm going to Joe as soon as I get back to the air center." She straightened her spine, and she could barely think around the fury running through her. "Hunter, you could've died."

"But I didn't. Don't borrow trouble." The conversation was over. At least for him. She pinched her mouth together, forcing herself to stay silent.

"Talk to Joe if you have to. I understand. But more important, I want you to be careful. Not just because I think Lance is dangerous for you personally, but because somebody has it out for him." His eyes softened again and for a moment he reminded her of the brother he used to be, so many years ago. She hadn't seen this brother much over the last decade. And if he wasn't strung up in traction right now, she might have thrown herself into his arms. She had missed him.

She nodded, unable to speak around the lump in her throat.

"Since I'm going to be stuck here for a while, I can't look out for you." He offered her grin. "Not sure who's going to keep you out of trouble now."

She tried to smile back. "I'll be careful."

"Good." He reached his good hand for her. She squeezed it, not wanting to let go. "I love you, sis. Not sure I tell you enough."

"You don't," she said. He barked a laugh. "But I love you too."

She glanced down at him. They had made a turn. After watching him be hurt, after how close she'd come to losing another loved one, she refused to leave things unsaid ever again.

"Bet you could use a snack. Hear the food in here isn't that great."

Her brother blew out a breath. "What I wouldn't do for a Snickers."

She extracted her fingers from his grip, and snagged her wallet on the way into the hallway. When she got there, she paused to lean against the wall.

She'd almost lost Hunter, and last night she'd finally come to terms with dating a firefighter, despite the danger they put themselves in every day.

But what Hunter described for Lance…could someone be trying to hurt him? It was bad enough that he was in constant danger due to firefighting, but this?

She would talk to Joe as soon as she got back. Lance hadn't told her. Probably planned to keep her out of it. If he thought she'd allow him to be in danger, he was mistaken.

Chapter 15

"I'm Special Agent Bates. Do you know why you're here?" Two days later, the officer from the Forest Services in front of him looked official and daunting. Lance had seen him arrive by plane earlier. He hadn't seen an official look so formal since the one that delivered the news that his father was dead and likely responsible for his jump partner's life.

Lance glanced around Mitch's office, taking in the dusty floor and general clutter, and wondered what the hell was going on. Mitch and Joe had taken up residence near the door and Meg looked out the window, her arms folded across her chest. He couldn't see her face, so there was no indication as to why he had been brought here.

"I can't say that I do." He could think of a few reasons, but all of them put his job at risk.

"I've heard you've been having some difficulty."

Well, wasn't that leading? "With training?"

"No. Mr. Buchanan tells me you're excelling there." The officer folded his arms over his chest. "He mentioned you had a few accidents."

Damn. So that's what this was about. He assessed the man in front of him. "Accidents, huh?"

The officer's eyebrows lifted. He leaned back on his hands, against Mitch's desk. Mitch wasn't going to like that. "What do you think they were?"

As far as he could tell, there were two options. He could pretend he didn't understand what any of this meant. The last weeks of stolen items, the ripped chute, the threatening letter. He'd have to hope that the man sizing him up with a shrewd look now believed that Lance was that clueless.

Except someone that naive shouldn't walk around unsupervised.

The pattern of incidents was clear. Someone was targeting him. It would take a special kind of stupid not to see that…the kind of stupid that didn't deserve to be one of the world's most elite firefighters. Surely the officer would doubt his competence. Lance would.

Which left him with the truth.

Lance couldn't think of any way around this. Across the room, Meg's guarded gaze studied him. He forced himself to watch her as he spoke.

"They aren't accidents." He swallowed. "I think someone knows I'm looking into my father's death."

Meg's fingers fluttered until they rested over her mouth, a failed attempt to hold in the gasp she made.

Though he was addressing the investigator, Lance refused to look away from her. "Last year, I read the investigative conclusions from the fire that killed him and Mr. Buchanan. My mother gave me the report. That my dad convinced Mr. Buchanan to jump on the wrong side. That you," he paused to look at Joe, "said they refused to leave before they were overrun." He turned his gaze back to Meg. "But, it doesn't make sense." He shook his head, feeling helpless against the betrayal on her face. "I need it to make sense."

Except that was a lie. He didn't only want it to make sense; he needed the truth.

"You think that someone did this to stop you?"

Lance narrowed his eyes on the ranger. Time to put all of his cards on the table. "Well, someone slashed a parachute I packed. I've had socks stolen, sneakers, a whole mess of personal items." It was annoying to have to run to Gram's house to get his things, but it had been easier than answering questions or being short on equipment. Maybe he should've said something. But he didn't want to be the guy whining. That might've been a mistake. By not taking that stuff seriously, maybe he'd driven whoever was doing this to do more dramatic things…like tangling a parachute that got his friend hurt. Glancing away, he took a deep breath. "I also got a threatening note. I thought it was a prank, like the stolen things. I didn't take it seriously." It was important that they understood that. If he'd believed, even for a minute, that this would lead to Hunter getting hurt…

"What?" Meg's voice broke. He'd kept so much from her, from everyone at the air center. He could only imagine what was going through her head right now.

"It's in my glove box. I'll give it to you when we're done."

The investigator grunted before pushing away from the desk. "Well, I'll admit, when Miss Buchanan called, I wasn't sure I should come. I was going to have them send me the parachute. It sounded like it could have been an accident. She didn't mention you were inquiring into your father's death."

"Because I didn't know." Her derisive response tore at him, and he gripped the handles on the chair tighter.

"Wait." Lance studied her. "You called the investigator?" No way. She had to know how much of a risk that put his job in. She wouldn't have done that…

"Did you know that Hunter Buchanan's parachute had been meant for you?" Mitch uncrossed his arms and leaned against the desk. "That you were the one who should've gotten the tangled chute?"

He glanced down, his jaw tightening. Damn it. Hunter had talked. "Yes. I knew."

Meg gripped her elbows, turning away from him.

"You should have said something, Mr. Roberts. These are very serious suspicions. Keeping them to yourself…you put everyone at jeopardy." The investigator swiped a file off the desk, his brows furrowed and frustration in his movements.

Lance's fingers flexed on the armrests, clenching and unclenching. Scanning the room, he tried to put himself in their shoes. "I never expected anyone to get hurt."

"Well, that's exactly what happened." The officer slapped the file back down. "We have the canopy. Someone tangled the lines. They're knotted. Someone did that on purpose."

Mitch interrupted, "Let's not panic. No one could've predicted it would go the way it had. The backup chutes…there was no way to guess that Hunter would lose his knife. And Lance had his. Maybe it was a careless prank."

"Maybe," the investigator said. "But it sounds like whoever is doing this is getting more brazen. Even the best-case scenario, that he tried to scare Mr. Roberts, isn't good. He didn't consider how bad it could go. Someone like that? They're dangerous." He gathered his things. "We need to root him out, before someone else gets hurt."

The investigator's resolve increased Lance's opinion of him. "What did you say your name was?"

"Bates."

"Thanks. I'll help however I can." He rolled all of the information around in his head, placing it against the other events of the past three weeks. Hunter had almost been killed. He didn't like being the target, but this had almost killed his friend. He couldn't take any more chances now. There were people he cared about at risk.

"You can make sure you speak up, if anything else comes up."

"Of course."

"No." Joe Buchanan pushed away from the wall. "Not just speak up. If anyone else gets hurt, you'll be gone. I can't have this kind of risk here. You must understand that."

It pissed him off. He'd done nothing but keep his head down and work hard. There were other guys who washed out, but not him. Yet even as he recognized that it wasn't fair, he could see where Joe was coming from. It was his job to keep everyone safe. Couldn't fault him for that. "I do understand."

Joe nodded. "Good."

"I'd like to take a statement, get your impressions of the things that have happened since you arrived. I'm going to talk to a couple of other people." Bates squared his shoulders. "We'll get to the bottom of this."

Mitch's expression was grim, and Joe looked sick. But Meg? She was pale, as white as milk.

This was everything she feared, everything she worried about. During their night together, he'd promised her that he would always be careful. But this was out of his control. He couldn't help that some psycho had targeted him.

How was he going to promise her that he would stay safe now?

He would have to talk to her. He would explain. They could do this.

He stood then, meeting eyes with the rest of them, so as not to make the moment awkward. "You'll let me know what else you need."

Bates nodded. "Tonight, come back here. I'll take your statement then."

"Sounds good." He needed to get out of here.

"But Mr. Roberts?"

He turned back, his hand on the doorknob. "Yes?"

"Be careful. This is a very dangerous situation. Don't be a hero."

Lance nodded, his gaze straying to Meg. She snorted, her face full of betrayal and anger. Through the ache of it, he recognized how unavoidable this had been. She was always going to find out that he was looking into their fathers' deaths. It's why he hadn't told her.

But her reaction? It wasn't only about the investigation. He'd lied to her. If it wasn't an outright lie, it was an omission of truth.

He'd pay for that. She might never trust him again. One thing was certain: he would never forget the look on her face right now. "Meg…"

She jerked her head, a barely noticeable shake. If her closed-off expression was any indication, the space between them now was miles wide. She turned away from him.

As he slipped into the hall, closing the door with a soft click, he exhaled. He should have known better. Except, he had. He'd only chosen to ignore what was inevitable—that she would hate him— to be with her for the time they had.

Now, that was over.

This might be for the best. Obviously, he was getting close. If Bates was right, the people around him could be in danger, too. Maybe this would keep her safe.

Because he wasn't going to stop. If this guy thought he could scare him, he didn't know him at all.

More, if someone was trying to stop him, it meant that he wasn't wrong to dig into his father's death. He must be closer than he thought.

* * * *

Following Lance out of the meeting was a mistake. Meg did it anyway. Apparently, she was glutton for punishment.

"Lance," Meg called as he hurried toward the exit. He didn't stop. "Lance!" He kept going, pushing through the door and into the field behind the air center. "Wait."

He halted, and she almost ran into him. He didn't turn. "Did you call in an investigator? Without asking me?"

Was he seriously mad at her right now? She propped her hands on her hips, glaring at him. "After everything you haven't told me? That's rich." She laughed. "Yes. I talked to Joe yesterday, when I got back from the hospital. Because I was worried about you." While she'd been worrying about him, he'd been lying to her.

"Why would you do that?" He hissed the words, glancing around, obviously not wanting anyone to hear their conversation.

"I needed to do something. To help. I hoped that if whoever is messing with you thought that they're being watched, they would think twice next time. I had no idea that you didn't care if someone was messing with you, that you didn't care how that might be putting everyone around you, including the other jumpers, at risk. Now that I know how much you've put yourself in danger, it seems I'm a little late to the party." She shook her head, swallowing. She was about to make a scene. Exhaling, she was determined to hold it together. "What were you thinking?"

"Seems pretty clear, doesn't it?" He buried his hands in his hair, gazing at the sky before turning to her. "I'm investigating our fathers' deaths. I have been since I got back. And I didn't tell you."

The words took the air out of her lungs. She could only stare at him. He was a stranger to her. All this time, after everything they'd been through since he returned? He had lied to her.

Hadn't everyone warned her? Her mom, Will, and even Hunter…her entire family. She hadn't listened, and now look at her. It was so predictable it was pathetic.

Except…it had to be impossible to fake emotion like that.

As she stared into his closed face, she couldn't find any traces of the man who had shared her bed. He'd worshiped her body, and his reverence had seemed genuine.

Then again, she had always been soft when it came to Lance. Maybe that's what she wanted to believe. She couldn't trust her own eyes when it came to him.

"Why?" She folded her arms around her, holding herself together. "Why didn't you tell me? You aren't the only one who lost their father. Don't you think I deserve to know?"

He snorted, his face cynical. "And what would you have said, Meg?" He made the motion for air quotes. "Sure, Lance, let's look into a cold case, dig up demons from a decade ago, from our past." He shook his head, giving a rude snort of laughter. "Demons from *our* past. That would've gone over great with your brothers. I'm sure they would be all for poking around in the past. Rehashing everything that went on all those years ago. They can barely look at me."

"Don't you think that was my choice to make?" He'd shut her out. Just like the last time, after his father died. He hadn't trusted her. It had hurt then, but this time? "It definitely wasn't Hunter's choice. He's in the hospital, because he got caught in your investigation."

"I never meant for anyone to get hurt."

His words were gritty and so honest, she had to look away from him. She clamped her lips shut, refusing to take it back. "I know." Lance might have lied, but he would never hurt anyone on purpose. "We're all just incidental contact." She laughed without humor. "Or maybe you need to admit that you're just as reckless as people believe you are."

He exhaled. "Meg…"

"What did you hope to find out?"

"Don't you think it's a little suspicious that three smokejumpers would all jump to the wrong side of the flames?" Lance buried his hands in his hair. "Your uncle might have been a newbie, but our fathers? They had been jumping for years. What was so different about this day? We are missing something."

"They made a mistake. People make mistakes." She took a couple steps back. "Just like this, between us. I made a mistake."

His mouth tightened. She wanted him to deny it. She wanted him to fight for them. Instead, he gave a short nod. "You're right. This was a bad idea. I knew I would hurt you. I should have never started any of this."

The words sliced. But she lifted her chin, and nodded back. "Well, I should have known better."

"For what it's worth, I'm sorry. I never meant to hurt anyone."

"Seems to run in your family. Destruction follows the Roberts men around."

He jerked. It was a low blow. She'd wanted to hurt him, though, as bad as she was hurting. She wanted him to strike out, like her. Then, maybe she would never feel anything for him again.

It would be easier to hate him.

But he said nothing. She bit back a scream, the urge to tell him to fight back. Her fists clenched at her side and she tightened her jaw, determined to stop. This was already pathetic, embarrassing. It's just that…it hurt worse than she expected it to. She'd prepared herself to lose him. When she chose to make love with him, she'd told herself that taking a chance on now was worth the risk to later. That the potential to lose him to the fires wouldn't outweigh what was between them now. But she hadn't expected this loss. She hadn't expected him to want to leave her.

She spun, unable to look at him any longer. He called for her, but she continued walking.

He'd hidden an investigation from her. She knew that he hated how things were in town, how people treated him, but he hid it well. Maybe he hated that more than the possibility of losing her.

Or maybe she didn't know him that well at all.

Inside, she grabbed her bag. As she slung it over her shoulder, Joe filled her doorframe. "You have a minute?"

The need to escape hummed through her, but she attempted a smile. "Can it wait? I was just going to run out."

"Not really. It's about Roberts." He pulled the door closed behind him. "I thought we should talk."

She clung to her purse strap, bracing herself. Of course, he'd want to talk. She hadn't exactly held it together in that meeting. "Yeah."

"Listen, Meg…" He shifted his weight. Joe had never been good at heart-to-heart conversations. "I know you guys were friends, growing up. I get that you might want to…rekindle that. But it looks…"

"Bad. You think it looks bad." Her stomach tightened. "How close we are. It isn't professional."

"No. It isn't." The corner of his mouth tilted up. "Have a care, that's all. I know how much you wanted to be here."

She had been so stupid. In her romantic fantasies, she'd believed they'd be able to work around all these complications. That all they'd need to do was get through training and then they could deal with the professional aspects of their relationship. Staring into her uncle's face, she could see how that had been naive. Almost as naive as trusting Lance. "Thanks, Uncle Joe."

He nodded and left.

She needed some air, to get out of here for a while. She shook her keys out of her purse and headed for the door. In the parking lot, she slid into her car.

She started to drive before she decided where she was going. She couldn't go to her mom's house. Not today. Not tonight. She'd go to Bend.

Decided, she turned up the radio, hoped it would drown out the noise in her head.

* * * *

That night, Lance left the air center later than he hoped. Like most of the days this week, Lance and the other recruits would jump twice between physical training sessions. The jumps were becoming more and more difficult, but he could handle it. He lived for the rush of floating through the sky. They were well into their third week, over halfway through their training.

After the day's training, he spent extra time cleaning and packing parachutes, doing his best to convince his teammates, his trainers, and himself that he wasn't the liability. But no matter how much extra work he did, nothing drowned out his conversations with the investigator and Meg. The guilt threatened to suffocate him.

He hadn't twisted that parachute, but if he'd spoken up…maybe if he'd said something sooner, Hunter wouldn't be in the hospital. The note, the tricks and stolen items…they had seemed harmless and his pride had kept him quiet. He hadn't wanted to be a tattletale. If he'd guessed those pranks would lead to this…

The investigator had asked him why he was looking into his father's death. While Bates assured Lance that he would include his search for answers into the larger investigation of what was going on at the air center now, he'd been clear that the old investigation into his father's death was completed. Obviously, Forest Services wasn't willing to reopen cases just to give him closure.

He threw his bag into the back of the Jeep, and slid into the driver's seat. Shoulders slumping, he gripped the wheel, staring out into the mountain. Was this what it would all come to? He'd spent all these years training, working out and preparing to be a smokejumper. Would he let his search for answers derail him inches from the finish line?

Part of him wanted to let it go. Move on. Was all of this worth it? If someone else got hurt...

He hadn't seen Meg for the rest of the day. He missed her. Now, in the privacy of his car, he allowed himself to feel that pain, without the constant eyes in the air center.

He'd done everything wrong with her. How he'd left things was eating at him. He'd barely slept last night, barely eaten. This morning, he'd told himself that he was fine. Here, though, alone...he admitted he wasn't.

It didn't matter. He couldn't apologize, couldn't ask for her forgiveness. Being around him right now...it wasn't safe for her. This way was the best, for her to stay far away from him.

Even as her loss was a physical ache.

He slammed his hand against the steering wheel, jammed the keys in the ignition and started up the Jeep. As he pulled out of the parking lot, he tried not to think about it. He was going to take tonight off. He'd take a drive, sleep at his grandmother's. Tomorrow he would figure this out, but tonight he couldn't get out of here fast enough.

He pulled out of the parking lot and accelerated. As he wound toward the main road, he took a deep breath and the last two days fell away.

The road became more winding, and he braked into a turn, continuing downhill. He'd been driving this road since he was a kid. He could do it with his eyes closed.

Except...suddenly, he was doing it without an engine. As he accelerated out of a turn, his car stalled, and took with it his power steering and power brakes. He wasn't entirely out of the curve though, and he couldn't get the wheel spun in time.

Seconds later, the Jeep hit the gravel in the shoulder and lost traction.

He did his best to pump the brakes and turn into the nose dive, but it was hard, and he didn't manage it soon enough. The tilt of the shoulder was too steep, and the Jeep slid sideways.

As the Jeep tumbled down the hill, the ground passed him twice in the window as the airbags deployed.

His heart pounded in his ears along with the beat from the radio. He did his best not to tighten up. Suffering an impact with stiffened muscles would cause more damage. Instead he tried to breathe, but even that was difficult.

He fell for an eternity. People say your life flashes before your eyes in moments of crisis, but that wasn't true. It was the people you loved that consumed your thoughts. His mom, Gram, and Meg...

With a sickening thud, the Jeep crashed, jerking him against the driver's door. Only his rapid pulse filled the resulting silence.

He didn't know how long it took him to be able to see anything outside his car. He pushed at the airbags, forcing them out of his way. When his vision cleared, the first thing he noticed was the giant tree trunk now embedded in the driver's side. Through the passenger's window, up the hill, the path of his descent was nothing but broken branches, fallen trees, and skid marks. He rubbed the side of his face, coming away with blood.

Great. As if his Jeep hadn't suffered enough, now he was going to bleed all over it.

He assessed the rest of himself, making note of a few aches, some scrapes, and a tender spot on his side from the seatbelt. But overall, he seemed fine.

Fine.

What the hell had happened? He just serviced his truck. He changed the oil himself, replaced the fuel filter, air filter. It was only a couple of years old. It didn't even have 20,000 miles on it. No way should it be stalling.

The inside of the cabin was a wreck. His gym bag had emptied out all over everything, dirty clothes and shoes scattered about. The contents of his glove box were all over the front seat. Luckily, he always kept his cell phone inside the middle compartment and that had remained closed. He popped the latch, finding the phone unharmed. He pressed the home button and it lit right up. Good. It still worked.

There was only one person he wanted to talk to right now. She might not want to hear from him. If it was him, he might not want to take his call. He hoped she was a better person than him.

He pressed recent calls, and hit send on Meg's number. When the line connected, his relief was so intense, he didn't greet her.

"I need help. I'm on McKenzie Highway. My Jeep went off the road." His voice was rough, full of gravel, like the stuff his truck had slipped in.

"My God. Are you okay?" Meg managed to fill her words with all of her worry.

For him, even after everything that had happened between them.

"I'm fine. I think." He laughed. "I haven't gotten out of the car yet."

"I'm going to call the police."

"Okay." With everything else going on, he couldn't shake the suspicion that this might not have been an accident. "But come, too? Please."

There was brief hesitation, then a sigh. "Of course."

The words loosened something in his chest. He closed his eyes, his jaw clenched.

Until now, the realization that someone was trying to sabotage him had been elusive. He couldn't pretend anymore, though. This could be some sort of freak accident, but he doubted it.

Someone was trying to kill him.

Was he putting Meg in danger? He'd already gotten Hunter hurt because of his decisions.

The pause on the line had become awkward. "Thanks, firecracker."

"See you soon." The line went dead.

He dropped his phone into the passenger seat, rubbing his now-aching neck. Maybe he should've told her not to come. Except he wasn't that strong. He needed her.

As he laid his head back against the headrest, he wanted to close his eyes—to rest—but he had enough medical training about head trauma to force his eyes open. He could have a concussion and he shouldn't go to sleep. He stared into the brush around him as he waited for the emergency personnel and Meg.

Chapter 16

"You could have stayed the night at the hospital, if you wanted." She touched the gash on his forehead and pretended not to notice when he flinched. Now, she hunched over him as he sat in a chair in her postage stamp kitchenette in Bend, smearing lotion on an abrasion on his arm and dressing it.

The place felt smaller with him in it. Maybe that was because all the things they were leaving unspoken were taking up all the space.

He offered her a wry grin, his face pale. "I don't need them to fuss over me. You're doing a great job."

Her hands stilled, mid cotton ball dab.

"Meg…" He ran his finger over her wrist.

She pulled away. Not because his touch disgusted her. The opposite.

At the sink, she washed her hands. "You could've been killed." If she'd been going for unaffected, she failed.

"People have been telling me that a lot lately." He probably wanted that to come out light, but it sucked the levity from the room.

She returned to the table, retrieving some medical tape. She wrapped a bandage on his wrist to cover the abrasion, shaking her head. "You know this isn't funny, right?"

He sighed. "I know, Meg."

"You aren't going to be able to hide this from Joe and Mitch and Bates, you know that too, right?" Because that was what she was afraid of, that he was going to try to downplay this. At this rate, he was going to get killed. She refused to not take that seriously.

"I know. I'm going to tell them tomorrow, let the chips fall." Meg could tell how much pain that caused him, and her fingers tightened.

"Who do you think is doing this?" She put down the ointment a little harder than she had to, and went to the sink to wash her hands. Standing too close to him wasn't helping her out of this conversation.

He exhaled, rolling his sleeve back over his arm. "I don't know. I don't have a lot of friends here anymore, but the only people who seem to actively hate me are Sledge and your brothers."

"No." Her stomach twisted, and she shook her head. This couldn't be her brothers. "Hunter…"

"I know. Definitely not Hunter." He grinned, but it didn't reach his eyes. "If he'd sabotaged a parachute, he would have remembered which one it was."

"No…" She breathed. Because that left Will. "Will…he wouldn't have done this. He might not like you but—"

Lifting his hand, he stopped her. "I know. I don't think it's him either. He's on the team. He wouldn't want to risk his job tormenting me. Personally, I think it's Sledge."

"Why?"

"You saw how he tried to antagonize me. I don't think he's above stealing my things or tormenting me."

"But the parachute? And this…accident." These weren't ordinary playground pranks.

"You don't think this was an accident either."

"Please. If it was the only thing going on, I might be able to write it off as an accident. But with everything else? No way."

He shrugged. "I don't know. The guy doesn't like me."

"Still, that doesn't mean that he's trying to *kill* you out of professional competition."

"Have any other suggestions then?"

"No. I don't." She shook her head. "Do you think it has something to do with you looking into…our fathers?" It was time to get this out of the way. As hard as talking about their fathers might be, it was probably easier than chatting about whatever else they weren't talking about.

Like how she loved him, and he was destroying her inside.

Pretty frightening when conversations about the past were safer than talks about what was happening now.

"Why don't I tell you what I know?"

A large part of her didn't want to know. A smaller, more cleverly-buried part did. Her stomach clenching, she shrugged.

"Okay." He nodded, inhaling as if to steady himself. "I convinced my mother to request the investigation report from the Forest Service a couple years ago."

Her exhale slid out, slow and smooth, and with it went all of the calm she'd built around herself for the past ten years.

"And?" she asked.

"The report stated that the spotter's radio caught our dads arguing before they jumped. Nothing incriminating and nothing definitive. Your Uncle Joe jumped right before them. They mentioned his name, and they argued about the wind. Somehow, they all ended up on the wrong side of the fire."

Her gut twisted, and she gripped the edge of the bench, rocking. The words tore at her chest.

"They argued and then jumped into the fire?" She shook her head. "That doesn't make any sense."

"I know." He tapped his knuckles on the table. "I've called a few of their old crew. One didn't give me any new information. I'm still waiting to hear from another, but the last said he would give me what he had, but I haven't heard from him."

"Did you talk to my uncle? He said he didn't remember much from that day but he was there. Maybe he'd have some insight." Even as she suggested it, thinking about her uncle having to relive that day…it squeezed her chest.

"No. I didn't." Shrugging, he offered a sheepish grin. "I didn't know how to ask. I figured it would come up, eventually, that there was no rush. I never expected to have to figure out who was trying to kill me."

"You don't think…my uncle…" She couldn't even voice the suggestion. What had happened over the past days that she would even consider that her family was capable of hurting others?

Lance shook his head. "He only found out yesterday that I was checking into the facts of the investigation. What would his motive have been?"

Nodding, she swallowed hard. That made sense, didn't it? If anything in this mess made sense anymore…

He pursed his lips, pausing. Finally, he said, "When I hear from our fathers' crewmates, would you come with me? To see them?"

"You want me to come? After you kept this from me?"

He stood, closing the distance between them. Tenderly, he took her hands in his and met her eyes. A shiver danced across her skin, sending heat to her stomach. "I shouldn't have done that. Keeping secrets from you…that was a huge mistake. I promise you, I won't lie to you again."

She wanted to believe him, more than anything else.

But did she want to learn more about what happened all those years ago? Her first reaction? No. Absolutely not. She didn't want to hear about their arguing or whatever decision-making process had sent her father careening into an inferno.

How was she going to explain that? "I'll come with you." The words came out more decisive than she expected.

"Great," he said, his smile wide. "I'll let you know."

"Still not sure what I can do for you." She hadn't done the research he'd done. All she was doing was tagging along.

"If you're asking questions about any of this, people will answer. This town feels for you, for your loss." He shrugged, his hands tucked away in his pockets. "No one wants to help me dig up information." He rocked forward, from the balls of his feet to his heels and back again.

She could only stare, and the truth of what he said seeped into her. He was right. If she asked any of her father's former teammates, they would help her, tell her anything she wanted to know. Everyone looked at her, her family, like victims.

They pitied them.

Lance would meet scorn.

As she stared up at him, she wanted to touch him. To squeeze his arm, to reach for his hand. Something to span the distance between them. Except if she touched him, she'd crumble. She'd forgive him, or she wouldn't care that she hadn't forgiven him. She'd fall into his arms, yet nothing would change.

She spun, leaning back against the sink on her hands. "What are the plans now? You're just going to keep looking into the fire, stay on at the air center?"

"I don't know, Meg." His voice was tortured, and she closed her eyes against it.

"What happens when one of these pranks puts you in the hospital next to Hunter?" That was a low blow, but from where she stood maybe that's how she had to fight. "I already almost lost one person I love to this."

Still unable to face him, she stopped there, the words floating in the air between them like smoke. Because she hadn't said it, not explicitly, but it was implied. She'd already almost lost somebody she loved implied she also loved him.

His hand gripped her forearm, turning her gently. He placed a hand on each side of her on the sink, pinning her between him and the counter.

Gazing down at her, his gray eyes burned into hers. "What are you saying?"

She couldn't hold his gaze. "I mean, I almost lost Hunter—I can't—it's so dangerous." She stumbled along until she ran out of words.

"No, not that part." His voice had dropped to a whisper, and his hand slid along her cheek, his fingertips rubbing her hair, behind her ear. "The other part."

"Oh, Lance." Unable to resist the warmth of him, she tilted her head into his palm, closing her eyes. She breathed out. "I can't believe it's a secret how I feel."

His lips fell on hers then, firm and insistent. He tilted her head as she gasped, using the opportunity to take her mouth more fully. His other hand curved around her back, pulling her against him, and she ran her hands up his back to hold onto his shirt. She couldn't get close enough to him. Maybe it was having him come so close to being seriously harmed today, or it could be that she would never be able to get enough of him. She didn't know. Either way, with him against her, things made sense. They felt right.

Kissing wasn't enough for long. He slipped his hands under her butt and lifted her. Wrapping her arms around his neck, she continued kissing him as he turned. He stumbled a little—thanks to his ankle—before he seated her on the table.

Swiping the medical supplies onto the floor, he coaxed her to lie back. As she broke their kiss, she whispered, "You think this can hold us?"

"We're going to find out." Reaching to the waistband on her yoga pants, he slid them and her panties off in one motion. Then he bent over and dropped his face into the junction of her thighs.

She gripped the edges of the tabletop as she cried out, her head tilted up to the light. God, he was so good with his mouth. As his lips and tongue played over the sensitive skin, his palms held her legs open. Splayed like this on the table, he had made her a feast.

As she got close to coming, she squirmed. "No, inside me. Please."

She didn't want to come the first time alone. As he stood, reaching for the button on his pants, his gaze was hot. There was a new level of intensity between them. Something about this sex was different than any of the times before. This time, as he slipped the condom on and slid between her legs, the connection between them was so intimate she couldn't look away. It would have been like abandoning him.

As he pressed inside her, she watched the play of emotions on his face and the vulnerability there was humbling. But when he began to move, she couldn't keep her eyes open, the pull of the sensations too much for her.

She allowed him to take the lead, letting herself get swept away by him inside her, his hands on her, and she tried to forget that when it was over, nothing would be different.

* * * *

The next morning when he arrived at the air center, Lance didn't say anything to anyone about his accident. He planned to talk to Joe and Bates first. But he couldn't exactly hide the stitches on his face. Or the fact that he was driving a rental.

"What happened?" Dak asked under his breath as they stretched in preparation for their morning run.

He glanced at his friend, his mouth thinning. Though the rest of them didn't deserve an explanation, he should have texted Dak. There were too many people around, though, so Lance only shook his head. "Later."

He wasn't going to get that lucky.

"I hear your truck had an unfortunate run-in with a tree yesterday," Sledge commented as he laced up his running shoes. "Sucks when that happens."

Lance tossed his track jacket into his cubby with more force than necessary. "You wouldn't know anything about that, would you?" Of everyone at the air center, Sledge had the most animosity toward him. He couldn't think of a better suspect.

The corner of Sledge's mouth turned up. "I have friends. EMT, volunteer firemen, policemen. They know who you are." Sledge got up, folding his arms over his chest. "Did you tell Joe or Mitch or anyone yet?"

Because he hadn't tracked them down yet, he deflected. "None of your business." He motioned to the room. "I'm here. I'm ready to work."

"Accidents follow you around, Roberts." Sledge shook his head.

"You should be thinking about our final test, not about me."

"What happens to you affects me." Sledge's usual snide look dissipated, leaving only seriousness. "As much as I hate to admit it, you're going to graduate." Lance wanted to add that he and Sledge were tied for top of their class, but he refrained. Sledge continued, "Whatever is going on with you affects us all. If you're in danger, you put us all at risk."

They stared at each other, and as much as Lance wanted to hate the guy—for his arrogance, his irritating way of being right all the time—he had to agree with him. He was right, both about the danger and its possible effect on the team. And as much as he hated to admit it, he had to admire that Sledge voiced his concern. If Sledge only cared about himself and his position in the team, he might be able to hate him. As he studied Sledge's face, he could see real concern there. He was worried about their teammates, and in that way, they had something in common.

"I have a meeting with Bates this afternoon. We're going to discuss what they find from the crash investigation." The words brought a fresh stab of shame. Lance hated that he was the one bringing this kind of drama and turmoil to their class. Behind the embarrassment was the always-present anger. This was bullshit. He didn't deserve to be dealing with this, but he didn't know what else to do.

Sledge nodded. "Good."

As they continued to stare each other down, Lance chuckled. The guy really was a piece of work. "Anything else I can do for you?"

"No," Sledge said, and then after a pause, he added, "Just for the record, though, I want you to know that this is messed up." He crossed his arms over his chest, his face twisting as if what he was about to say didn't agree with his stomach. "I don't like you, no secret. But—" he shrugged. "You work hard, and you're one tough, stubborn asshole. You've proved to me that you deserve to be here. So whoever's fucking with you...if we find out who it is, he'll answer to me, too."

Without another word, he grabbed the rest of his workout gear and strolled out, leaving a mixture of stunned silence and chuckles in his wake.

Well, didn't that take the cake? Lance had wondered more than once if Sledge had something to do with all of the accidents around him. He still wasn't sure the guy was in the clear, but their conversation proved once again that there was no telling what was going on in someone's head.

Dropping the rest of his things, he decided not to put this off any longer. Striding into Joe's office, he knocked on the doorframe. "Joe? You got a minute?"

The base manager glanced up. He took in the stitches on Lance's face, the bandage on his arm. "I do."

"There was an accident last night. My Jeep. We should talk." The words stuck in his throat.

Joe's mouth firmed and then he nodded. "The police detective called earlier. After your run this afternoon, come back. We'll talk before you meet with Bates."

He rapped his knuckles on the door again. "Right. Sounds good."

As he returned to his spot, he wondered if today would be his last day of training.

Chapter 17

Meg was running late.

She led the recruits on their afternoon run, and she couldn't help the burst of pride she had in them. Over the past four weeks, they'd all improved tremendously. Their endurance had increased, they'd slimmed down, and all of their times were better now.

Lance had avoided her eyes for the majority of the day, his movements efficient but jerky, as if he was irritated. She wondered what was going on even as she tried not to let her imagination get out of control. He was dealing with a lot right now. Surely, he was entitled to be distracted.

The weather was getting warmer and she worked up a real sweat, so she grabbed a quick shower before she was supposed to meet with Joe.

She twisted her wet hair into a bun and wondered what this was about. Mitch had made a few comments recently that he might not want to do this again next year. She wondered if Joe was going to approach her to take Mitch's spot. She tried not to get her hopes up, though. This was only her first year. She had no idea if there were other more seasoned applicants. Still, her heart picked up.

As she twisted the knob and opened Joe's office, though, any chance this meeting was about a promotion flew out the window.

The gathered group looked just like the one earlier this week when investigator Bates had arrived. He stood next to Joe's desk, his face grim. Joe and Mitch were also in attendance, and Lance had taken up the seat in front of Joe's desk again.

Fear twisted her stomach, making her nauseous, and reminding her she hadn't eaten much at lunch today. She hadn't eaten much over the past two days, actually.

What had happened now? She couldn't help scanning Lance for any new bruising or injury. She hated that she did that. She wondered if she'd ever be able to stop now. Would she always be waiting for the next time he got hurt?

She shied away from that. This wasn't the time to be exploring all of the concerns in her relationship.

Stepping inside, she closed the door quietly behind her. "Sorry I'm late."

"No problem," Mitch said. "I told them you'd been out on a run."

Lance mustn't have stopped for a shower, because he still wore his workout clothes and his hair was still damp. Even so, or maybe because of, he looked as sexy as ever.

She glanced around the room. "What's this about?"

Joe sighed. "I'll let Mr. Bates explain."

Bates picked a file folder off of Joe's desk, but he didn't take anything out of it. "These are the results of the investigation into Mr. Roberts's crash yesterday. According to diagnostics on his vehicle, there was an unusually large amount of sand in his fuel tank." He put the file back down on the desk. "The sand contaminated the fuel filter, causing the vehicle to stall, and resulting in the loss of Mr. Roberts' power steering and power brakes. The confluence of all of those factors caused his accident."

"Sand in my fuel tank." Lance's face remained expressionless. "Someone contaminated my Jeep."

The ramifications stole Meg's breath. No one would put sand in someone's fuel tank without wanting to cause them trouble. "What does sand in the fuel tank usually do?"

"It wreaks havoc on an engine, obviously," Lance said, his jaw tight, his voice sharp. "Most of the time it would cause the engine not to start. But, in this case, whoever did this either meant to hand me a large mechanics bill, or—"

"Or they hoped something worse would happen to you." Bates tilted his head in agreement. "Worse than what happened to you, I should say."

Lance nodded. As he didn't react, Meg could only stare at him.

They'd suspected as much, but hearing it confirmed…

"Do you have any suspects?" There had to be something. No one had seen anything? The air center parking lot was busy. How had someone done this without anyone knowing?

"We're still in the process of questioning people. So far, I don't have anything to report." Bates' mouth thinned. It bothered him, too, then.

"There have to be other resources we can tap. The police, can we get other federal officers involved? This is a government agency. No one should be able to threaten one of our officers and get away with it." There had to be something they could do that they weren't doing. Someone must be dropping the ball somewhere.

She caught Lance's eye, though, and he shook his head. He didn't want her to push. She clamped her jaw closed, looking away. He was right.

The more she said, the more she gave away her true feelings for him. From Mitch's suspicious gaze, to Joe's averted glance, she was on thin ice.

"We're installing security cameras throughout the premises, including the parking lot. That should deter much of the monkey business." Bates knocked on the desk, right over the file. "But I can't express how important it is for you to be careful, Mr. Roberts. If you notice anything out of the ordinary, you need to let one of us know immediately."

"Of course." Lance rubbed his palms on his thighs. "Anything else?"

Joe inhaled, and foreboding laced down her spine. "I want to talk to you about your plans after training."

Lance's brow creased. He didn't like this either. "What do you mean?"

"This isn't usually how it's done, but I've spoken with Bates and he agrees." Joe cleared his throat with an awkward cough. "It might be better if we transferred you to another team." As that bombshell dropped in the middle of the room, Joe hurried on as if to make sure no one cut him off. "Bates thinks that if we explained the situation, one of the other smokejumper teams might be willing to swap for you."

"You want me to leave?" Lance's calm voice gave nothing away, but she knew better.

"Not leave exactly. We don't want to lose your expertise, and you're a damn fine firefighter. The Forest Service needs you." Mitch hurried to explain. "We only wanted to offer a solution. If you were interested."

"I'm not. If you want me to go, you're going to have to fire me. I'm not letting some nameless punk scare me out of here. I have as much of a right to be here as any of these other guys."

"I'm not sure you're going to have that choice." Joe straightened some papers on his desk, before looking up at Lance. "If we can't discover who is doing this soon, we will need to act in the best interest of the team. This isn't about you. Someone doesn't want you here. Until we find out who that is, it might be best if you aren't here, either."

"You might never find out who it is." Lance's tone was sharp. "If I'm gone, and this guy fades away, then I'll have had to move and the person responsible will never be brought to justice."

Joe lifted his hands, shaking his head. "I understand your frustration, but unless something happens soon to prove to all of us that you aren't a danger or aren't in danger here, we might not have any other choice."

Lance wanted to argue, she could see it on his face. His jaw was tight, and his fists were clenched, but he kept his mouth shut, nodding.

Her temper spiked. Part of her understood. Joe had to look out for the entire air center, and if he needed to neutralize the situation for now until they could find out more information, she got that. But the part of her that cared about fairness, the part that hated when kids peeked during games of hide and seek or when someone cheated on a test in school, that part of her was outraged.

Not to mention that Lance would be gone.

"There has to be more we can do." She motioned toward Mr. Bates. "I get that you're doing your job, but maybe if we had more resources, more investigators. There has to be something else besides this." She refused to look at Lance, afraid she would give herself away. But that didn't keep her from defending him. "It isn't fair."

"Fair or not, we have to do what keeps everyone safe."

She opened his mouth to argue, but Lance cut her off. "I understand. Our final jump is in two days. Hopefully we will have more information by then."

He shook his head the slightest at her, and she got the message loud and clear. She glared at him. This wasn't right. It bothered her that they weren't going to pursue this further. But it was up to him.

Why wasn't he sticking up for himself?

As she followed him out of the office, she waited until they were alone in the hall and grabbed his arm, stopping him. "Why didn't you say more back there? This isn't fair."

"You're right. But, this isn't about fair." Lance's brow was low, his eyes hard. "Things aren't fair sometimes, Meg. I know that better than most." He turned as if he was going to walk away, but she grabbed his arm again.

"What does that mean?" She hissed. "What are you trying to say?"

"You...maybe things always work out for the best for you. Maybe whatever is right, whatever is just...maybe those things happen for you. But if I've learned anything since our fathers died, it's that sometimes you have to take the punches when there's nothing else you can do."

"That's bullshit."

They stared at each other, at a crossroads. Was he going to let them chase him out of here? Then again, he'd left before. Maybe this wasn't worth fighting for to him.

Maybe what they were doing together wasn't worth fighting for either.

Her anger seeped away, leaving only a bone-crushing loss. "If you leave here, where are you going to go?"

"I don't know, Meg." He sighed, his hands on his hips. It was asking a lot right now, but she needed a clear picture of where she stood with him. "I don't think they know."

"So you'll just take that chance?" She hated what was she was about to say. "You'll leave here? Again? You'll leave me." Her pain was clear in her voice, but she'd never been good at hiding her feelings.

"Meg..." He shook his head. "It's not like I have a choice. You heard them. If they think I need to go, there's not much I can do about it."

If she argued with him, if she made a case for why he should fight to stay when he might be in danger or put others in danger, she would look selfish. Be selfish. But it wasn't like her not to fight for what she wanted, for the people she cared about. Could she fight for him, when he wouldn't fight for them?

There was only so much she could do.

She looked down, into the corner...anywhere to avoid looking at him. "Right. Of course."

"Meg..." He reached for her, but she moved away. She couldn't handle it if he touched her right now.

"No, it's okay. I get it." She backed up, determined to hold it together here, in their workplace.

She was an idiot. Had she believed that he'd changed, that he'd suddenly become the man who stayed and fought when things were hard?

"Why don't you just text me later?" She motioned behind her, toward her office. "I have to get back to work."

She attempted to walk away, to retain any dignity. But he stopped her. "Meg?"

"Yeah?"

"I'm meeting someone. About our fathers." He exhaled, as if he didn't want to tell her this. "I told you I'd let you know, so you could come with me."

"Right." She glanced back at him.

"Would you like to come?"

She didn't. But, she couldn't pretend she didn't want to know what was happening. He wasn't going to tell her on his own. If she wanted information, she needed to go along with him, hear for herself. "Sure. When?"

"Tonight."

"Fine. Let me know."

Chapter 18

Lance trailed behind Meg as they followed the directions Roger Palance's wife had given them, around the back of the house and out into the garden.

He'd picked her up at Stack Park a half an hour ago. The conversation on the way north to the Palances' house had been equal parts stilted and overly friendly.

Meg was trying too hard. Her smile was too wide, her back too straight. He didn't know what to do to calm her down, so he'd allowed her to talk until she ran out of gas. He answered her questions, asked about her day. When she couldn't find anything else to say, he offered to let her choose the radio station. They'd driven the rest of the way with the country station filling the silence, both of them lost in their own thoughts.

Maybe he should have let her drive separately. He'd been afraid she might not come, though. He'd also refused to deny himself the opportunity to sit in her company. Call him selfish, but he would rather have an uncomfortable car ride with her than drive alone.

Now, they walked around the house and down a stone path to the garden. Roger knelt in the dirt, a straw hat pulled over his eyes.

He must have heard them coming because he glanced up before returning to his work. "You two are ten years too late."

Lance didn't know if he'd ever met Roger. He'd heard his name lots of times growing up. His dad always said he was subtle as sandpaper. Guess he could understand that now. "I'm sorry, sir?"

"If you wanted to ask questions, you're a decade late." Roger tugged at an overgrown shrub of some kind. "Not sure what anything I say now will help."

"We appreciate the help anyway." He'd called, so Roger had been aware he was coming. But he hadn't told him anything about bringing Meg. Roger's wife hadn't mentioned any loss of faculties, but maybe the guy thought they were someone else.

Roger snorted. "You're the spitting image of your father."

Lance grinned at him. "I've heard that before."

"I bet." He leaned back on his knees, shielding his eyes from the early evening sun. He pointed at Meg, his face softening. "And you? You've got the look of your mother, with your father's coloring." He tipped his hat. "You're the Buchanan girl."

Meg shifted, obviously uncomfortable.

Lance stepped closer, taking the attention away from her. "You called, said you had some information for us."

"That I do." Roger shifted, getting to his feet faster than most sixty-year-olds Lance knew. Then again, the guy had spent his entire adult life in top physical shape, chasing fires up and down the Western part of the US. He dusted his hands off on his pants. "Come on. Regina made cookies because you were coming. Doesn't make me cookies. Blood sugar. Let me get you both a drink. Beer?"

They followed him to a set of patio furniture situated under a huge fir tree. Roger reached into a cooler, pulled three Coors out. He accepted one and popped the top.

Meg waved hers off. "No, thank you."

Roger motioned to the cooler. "Tea?"

"I'm fine."

Lance didn't know why she turned it down, but she looked pale, her face drawn. The old Meg wouldn't turn down cookies either, but she left the plate untouched. He furrowed his eyebrows at her when Roger turned his back, questioning, but she only shook her head.

Roger lifted his beer, and Lance tapped it with his own before taking a drink. Roger motioned to the chairs next to him. "Please."

"That's okay," Meg smiled, but her mouth was tight. "I'll stand, if that's okay with you." She looked antsy, as if she'd prefer to pace around.

"Suit yourself." Roger shrugged, dropping into one of the chairs.

Well, Lance wasn't going to stand if he didn't have to. His whole body was aching from training, not to mention his bad jump with Hunter and his car accident. Besides, Meg seemed like she might not want to be watched too closely. So, he sank down, giving her some space to move around.

As he settled, he glanced across the property. He'd forgotten, having been away from Oregon so long, how beautiful the landscape was. He sipped again, shifting his shoulders, allowing the stress to roll off him.

"You want to know about your fathers."

He didn't have to see Meg fully to feel her stiffen. He glanced to the side at the older man, but Roger wasn't watching either of them, staring out in the direction he'd been looking. Lance returned his gaze there as well. It really was breathtaking. "Yes. Were you there that day? On the plane?"

Roger chuckled. "You can't start there, my boy. That misses the point, doesn't it?"

Another sip of beer. "What do you mean?"

The lines around Roger's eyes creased deeper. "The two of them. Jason and JT, your fathers…starting on the plane misses everything that matters." He took a long drink of his beer before resting his forearms on the arms of the chair, his hands hanging over the ends. "They were jump partners. Folks in this town might want to blame your dad, but the two of them…" He shook his head. "Nothing good or bad could happen to only one of them. They were together in all of it, through thick and thin."

So much had happened since those days. Lance could barely remember the time before the Blue Creek fire. But he remembered Jason Buchanan. He and his father were more like brothers than friends. His more charismatic father, always the life of the party and thrived in a crowd. Jason, Meg's father, was more subdued, but with a spine of steel. Like Meg, actually.

"I piloted that day. JT and Jason were the last pair to go. They jumped after your Uncle Joe and his partner." He stared ahead, as if lost in the memory. "I didn't see them jump. I only noticed when their parachutes took off in the wrong direction. Joe got twisted in it all, but managed to land a mile away. When we found him, he was unconscious. JT and Jason landed in the danger zone."

He knew the specifics after that. They'd found his father and Jason Buchanan two days later. The coroners listed the official cause of death as smoke inhalation.

"What was on the coms?" The smokejumper spotter wore a headset.

Roger paused, reaching into his pocket. He pulled out a thumb drive, holding it out to Lance. "This is for you."

The tech looked strange in Roger's elderly fingers. "What is this?"

"The recordings of that day. From the plane."

Lance's fingers closed over the drive. This is what he had been hoping for. A new lead.

"Lance?"

He turned, making eye contact with Meg. He couldn't read her expression, but the turmoil in her eyes cut through him.

"For what it's worth, son, I don't blame your father." There was a new softness in Roger's tone, before he addressed Lance again. "I don't know who made the mistakes in what happened up there, but I know one thing for sure: Jason was no victim. They didn't make decisions without each other. Ever." He took a long drink from his can, settling deeper into his chair.

Did that mean whatever happened had been both of their faults? People in town assigned blame, years ago. JT had been the first one out of the plane. Fact. Jason followed him. In the middle of the chaos, they'd almost taken Joe down with them, and he'd only survived by some miracle he couldn't remember.

He studied Roger. If he said that JT and Jason made their decisions together, what did that mean? He filed the info away, finished his beer, and stood. "Thanks for seeing us on such short notice."

"Yes," Meg added. "Thank you. I'll just run in and thank your wife for the cookies." She nodded to Roger and smiled, but Lance could tell it was strained, fake. She headed toward the house, her head down. She was hurting. He wanted to follow her, but Roger's words distracted him.

"Hear you're in this year's rookie class," he said as he got to his feet.

Lance stilled, wondering where this was going. "Yes, sir."

"With the middle Buchanan boy."

Funny that he called them boys. They were in their mid-twenties. "Yes, sir."

Roger nodded toward the house where Meg had just disappeared. "Imagine they weren't happy to see your face."

"No warm and fuzzy welcome, if that's what you mean." Even as he said the words, they weren't fair. Meg had been different.

"Huh." Roger shrugged, gazing after her. "Be patient. They haven't had an easy road either."

Lance nodded, but part of him rebelled. They hadn't had an easy road? They hadn't been shunned after it happened. The way the town had treated his mother? If they'd had leprosy, more people would have talked to them. Instead, it had become so isolated, his mother had preferred to cut ties and go instead of dealing another minute.

"I'm serious." Roger cast a glance at him from under his straw hat. "None of them remain unaffected. From Karen on down through the twins."

Lance shouldn't have been surprised. Obviously, there was a lot Roger kept to himself.

When he didn't go on, Lance forced himself to keep his trap shut. He didn't trust what he'd give away. This was still a small town, and the air center community—past and present—was a tight-knit one.

"Good luck." Roger held out his hand, and Lance shook it. "I'm going to offer you some advice, even though you didn't ask."

Lance laughed. Roger struck him as the "ask forgiveness, not permission" sort.

"Leave the past alone." He clasped Lance on the shoulder. "You aren't your father, no matter what anyone might try to do to convince you otherwise."

There was no use in arguing with him, but that was easier said than done.

He thanked Roger and headed to the house to get Meg. Roger's words about the Buchanans echoed in his mind. They had changed. Will was angrier, Hunter more brooding. Meg…of all of them, Meg's change might be the subtlest, but he could still see it. She was quieter, more thoughtful. More restrained.

He reached into his pocket, fingering the thumb drive. He wondered if this would help…or ruin everything.

* * * *

"Should we listen to it now?" The thumb drive lay in the middle console, making Meg nervous. They were still parked in the Palance driveway. Considering she had no idea what they would find, she didn't know if this was the appropriate place for major revelations about their fathers. "Why don't we wait until we're back to Stack Park?"

Lance nodded, as if he understood her reservations. They drove in silence. As she stared out the window, she tried to run through how bad this could be. What could it possibly say? If the original reports had been inconclusive, there was nothing on that thumb drive that would prove otherwise. So why would Mr. Palance give them this information?

As the tension continued, she started to wish that she would have refused when Lance asked her to tag along. Whatever they heard on those transmissions could change everything.

They parked in their usual spot at Stack Park, and Meg inhaled, bracing herself as she reached for the drive and plugged it into the USB port in the rental. Might as well get this over with. She turned up the volume, and waited.

Neither of them looked at each other as the transmission of the day their fathers died wafted through the speakers. The recording was exactly what she expected radio transmissions from a decade ago to sound like: gritty and barely understandable. They listened as the rudimentary motions of a fire jump recited through the car. And then...

"Buchanan!" Hearing someone call her name struck her through the gut.

"That's the wrong side of the flame." Meg couldn't tell who was talking, but whoever it was sounded panicked. More than that, they sounded outraged.

The next bit was garbled, full of shouting. "We need to go. On the east."

Erupting from the speakers, Lance's father sounded exactly as she remembered, like a voice from the grave.

"That's the wrong side," Jason Buchanan's steady timbre answered, and she covered her mouth. "It's wrong."

"No, the west, Roberts. Go."

That was the spotter, Ken Wassy. He'd passed away two years ago.

There was more garble. Then, JT again. "We follow."

After that, the yells erupted again, all speaking over each other.

From there, they listened as the pilot and spotter relayed back to the air center that three jumpers were going the wrong way. There was anger and fear, questions filled with concern.

Two days later, rescuers would find their fathers dead.

The remainder of the flight recording gave them nothing new. Eventually, Lance turned it off. The silence in the rental was heavy. "Lance..."

"Stop." He closed his eyes. "I can tell what you're going to say. A lot of crap about how it's not as bad as it sounds. You heard it, though. That's not true."

She chose her words carefully. "I'm not sure what I heard."

"That was obviously my father, Meg." His eyes found hers in the dying light, and the pain there burned through her. "You know that as well as I do. I'm not an idiot."

"Yes, but..." It wasn't as clear as that. His father had mentioned jumping on the wrong side, but he didn't explain why.

"There are no buts. There's nothing here. Nothing that changes what we didn't already know. That was my dad, talking your dad into jumping on the east side."

"Yes," she said. "It was." There was no denying that truth. "But there was so much yelling, and not all of it was clear. Our fathers—" she glanced at the sunset. "They could speak without saying words. Like you and Hunter used to. There's so much that could have been said without talking."

She didn't know what else to tell him. If they had heard something that went against the investigation's conclusions, Lance would keep looking. It would be safer if he gave this all up. If he stopped investigating, maybe whoever had it out for him would leave him alone. Maybe he would stay in Redmond, and they could be together.

But that wasn't true. Because she wasn't sure he would stay if there was no change in the report's conclusions. Would he stay if everyone still assumed his father was a reckless and endangering firefighter? Would he ever be able to step out from behind that shadow?

Watching him learn nothing new was tearing her apart.

"We can keep looking." She reached out, gripping his forearm. She wanted to tell him everything she felt inside. That she loved him. That it didn't matter what his father had done, that he wasn't his father. But he was gone, sitting in the driver's seat next to her. And she had never been so helpless.

"Sure. Yeah, we can keep looking." He lifted his arms to grip the steering wheel, effectively breaking their contact.

She had resigned herself to the fear of losing him to the fire, but she had never expected to lose him to himself.

He started the Jeep, and they drove the short distance back to the air center in silence.

Chapter 19

The morning of the last training jump dawned bright and cold. Even though it was the end of May, the recruits put extra layers on under their high-collared jumpsuits. There was rain predicted later, though, which meant the wind was picking up.

No one spoke. Since Bates arrived at the center, any levity had been sucked out of the air. Most of them probably hoped that when they were fully minted, they would be safe from whatever danger was following Lance around. As if the end of training would equal the end of their troubles. Lance wasn't so sure.

Each of them packed their pockets and silently checked each other's parachutes. As they loaded into the plane, the distance between him and the rest of the team was palpable.

After this, he would face the future, the possibility that he would be leaving the air center. It wasn't the worst option since his family history in Redmond made it hard for him to connect here. And after all the "accidents" he'd suffered through, the rest of the guys steered clear. He killed cohesion, and it might just be best if he left.

After what he had heard last night on Palance's recording, he'd been forced to admit this had been a fool's pursuit. His father had definitely convinced Jason Buchanan to jump on the wrong side. He didn't know why. Arrogance, probably. The Roberts men seemed to be saddled with it. Look at him. That was the only explanation for why he thought he could change things here.

Keeping after his investigation into his father was pointless.

Meg's face flickered in his mind, her perfect features. He'd ruined it with her. Circumstances at training and in town might be out of his control, but he'd put the space between him and Meg. He'd created that divide and now all of his reasons to stay were gone.

Maybe the best thing he could do now was land this jump, and then show Redmond the back of him.

They ascended to their jumping altitude, the engines and wind sound drowning any other thoughts. The plane hit a bunch of turbulence, but none of them would be here if rocky trips into the sky bothered them. This jump would mimic the most complicated conditions. They would fall into dense vegetation on sloped ground. Outside, the breeze was strong, but nothing unmanageable. He checked his gear one more time and nodded to Rock. They would be partnered this time.

Except, when Tim stood up in front of them, he shook his head. "Change of plans. We're going back."

"What?" Next to Lance, Sledge screamed over the engine noise. "Why?"

"Lightning strike, twenty miles from here." Tim pointed, farther north. He turned to the pilot. Lance couldn't hear what they discussed, but it didn't take much calculation to see what was happening.

If they turned back, away from the lightning strike, they would backtrack. It would cost the veteran smokejumpers an hour they didn't have. A lightning strike, even with the possibility of rain coming, was incredibly dangerous. The rain levels had been lower than average this spring, leaving dry conditions behind. Who knew what kind of damage would be done while they returned to the base or how far the fire would spread in that time?

Lance studied the men around him. All of them looked frustrated, too. This wasn't what they'd trained for, to let fires burn while they flew around, paralyzed by bureaucracy. They hadn't finished their last jump, but they were ready. They were already here, and they were dressed to fight this. There were four recruits and four seasoned jumpers on the plane now, they could drop first, do their best to subdue the blaze while the pilot returned for backup.

He stood, weighed down by all of his gear but determined. "We can do this," he yelled at Tim. "We should go. To the strike point."

"I don't know..." Tim shook his head. "You haven't finished—"

"If we wait, it gets bigger." It was loud and there wasn't time for a lot of words. Through the cage of his helmet, Lance held the trainer's eyes, trying to say what would be too hard to yell. It was the same thing on every other recruit's face in the plane. They could fight this blaze.

Tim looked over his shoulders, probably to the other four veterans. Finally, he nodded. His jaw firm, he clasped Lance on the shoulder. "Yes. We go."

Lance sat back down as Tim turned to fill in the pilot. A zing of adrenaline shot through him, drowning out the sound of the engine accelerating. This was what they trained for, and they were ready.

Less than five minutes later, the streamers that read the wind direction were lobbed out of the open plane door. Below, they swayed, signaling a westward blow. Tim stood, scanning the blaze beneath them. "We jump to the back and attack from the right." He motioned. "Land there."

They all nodded. He pointed at Sledge. "Go."

Sledge moved into the door. He waited for Tim's slap on the shoulder, and when it came, he launched into the air. Dak followed him out. After them, Tim sent two of the veterans, including Will. Then, it was Lance's turn.

He sat in the door, waited for his pat on the back, and threw himself out into the wind.

The fire wasn't big, but it already had a bite. It oscillated in the breeze slowly, like it was doing the hula. The burn swirled as if to say, *I'm calm now, but soon I will rage.*

As he turned his attention to steering and finding a landing position, he spied a cabin tucked behind the trees. He lost sight of it as he maneuvered his parachute, but the stakes increased exponentially. If there was anyone in there, they needed to get them out. The fire would march over it. The hair on his arms stood up.

They'd been right to come.

He landed without hitting a tree—thank God—and gathered his parachute, already stripping out of his jumpsuit. As he stowed his gear, he prepared to fight the flame, like he'd been taught. Lizard, the most senior veteran among them, joined him. He yelled to him over the fire. "There's a cabin. Did you see it?"

Lizard nodded, his mouth grim. "It's in the path."

Lance glanced toward the smoke in front of him. "I can go. Around. Check it." It was a request, because technically, Lizard was in charge. He could choose to release him to go or not.

"It's too dangerous. We still don't have a good read on how fast this one is moving."

"I know. But it's more dangerous for anyone stuck inside that cabin."

Lizard glanced at the flames once more, then toward the cabin. "Take Will. You two are the fastest runners." He narrowed his eyes on Lance. "Do you have your shelter?"

They all carried the aluminum and fiberglass tent-style shelters, designed to give a wildland firefighter a last resort to protect themselves against the flames.

He nodded. "Of course." After what happened to his father—that he and Jason Buchanan were found sharing one, the other missing—there was no way he'd ever leave it behind.

"Good." He turned to Will, his jump partner. "Buchanan. You're going to go check out that cabin with Roberts."

Lance didn't make out Will's exact words, but his tone was sharp. Obviously, he wasn't pleased with getting paired with Lance. Lizard's rebuke said he wasn't hearing any drama today. "I don't care what's between your families. You guys do your job and get back safe, got that, rookie?"

"Loud and clear."

"Good. Then, go."

As Lance set off at a run, Will fell in behind him. Lizard was right. They had work to do. Their history didn't matter right now.

At the base of the hill where he was certain he'd seen the cabin, he paused. Catching his breath, he shielded his eyes from the sun. The burn wasn't more than a few hundred yards behind them, moving toward the cabin fast. "I think it's up there, beside that outcropping of rocks."

Will nodded, not making eye contact. Lance rolled his eyes. Great. They were supposed to be a team, and the guy wouldn't even look at him. He forced his frustration down, refocusing on his work.

He hurried, scrambling up the embankment in front of him. Rounding the rock cove he'd spotted, his throat tightened, his stomach churning. The cabin was here, all right. In front of him, the flames had already found the cabin. A man stood with a fire extinguisher, trying to force them back, but it was like David and Goliath. Inside, he heard crying.

"There's someone in there," he yelled to Will. "We need to go." He started to run toward the cabin. Will stepped in front of him, pushing him in the center of his chest to stop him.

"No, you need to stay. I'll go in, and you go to help the man."

"There are people inside, Will."

"And I don't trust you. We split up. You help him. I'll get them myself."

Lance would have argued any other time. But, it was clear that the man needed help and even more apparent that Will wouldn't accept his. That he would never accept him.

Lance turned away, sprinting across the field. He unstrapped his gear, preparing to remove the brush and fuel from the fire's path, their only chance to buy Will and whoever was inside any time. "Keep the spray on the burn. I'll do what I can to make a line."

Even as he threw his back into the physical labor, the adrenaline of being so close to the flames humming through his blood, he couldn't hide from reality. They shouldn't have split up. It was more dangerous this way.

If the team didn't trust him—even a few of them—then how was he supposed to do his job?

He ratcheted up his effort, digging and cutting in a frenzy.

The sound of splintering wood sliced through the air, and Lance paused, turning toward the cabin. The scene in front of him was straight out of a horror movie.

Against the backdrop of swirling flames around them, the house collapsed from the middle in, like a balloon deflating.

Chapter 20

"What do you mean they're lost?" Meg paced in front of Joe's desk. "What happened?"

"I'm still waiting on details, Meggy." Joe pointed to his cell phone on the desk next to him. "The guys in the tower will call me. That's how this works."

He'd told her that already, but she couldn't sit still. She'd come in, even though she didn't have to today, because she wanted to finish her talk with Lance. She didn't care if he didn't have anything else to say, she wasn't done with this. She refused to give up on them.

But, the morning had gone from waiting for the jumpers to return, so she could talk with Lance, to something out of her worst nightmares.

"There are only four seasoned jumpers in that group. They aren't prepared, don't have the gear for this specific fire." She paced, unable to sit down or stand still.

"I know. They have enough to get started. Pete and Tim are coming back with the plane. They'll go back then, and take the rest of the jumpers and equipment with them."

On the desk, his phone buzzed. Joe lifted his finger to her, giving his attention back to the phone at his ear. He made a bunch of appropriate grunts, meant to tell the speaker he was following along. Then he said, "They did? Okay. Keep me posted."

He lowered the phone, disconnecting. "The fire's still burning, but they have it under control. There's a bigger issue. Lizard sent Will and Lance to check what he thought was an abandoned cabin on the hill behind the lightning strike." Joe shook his head. "They haven't come back yet."

"No." Will and Lance, both unaccounted for. Her pulse beat loud and hollow in her ears. "They're okay, though, aren't they?"

His eyes were sympathetic. She hated it. "I don't know yet. Lizard sent someone to check on them."

She buried her hands in her messy ponytail. Probably looked like a crazy woman. Matched how she felt. "Why are they even there in the first place? This was supposed to be the last training jump. What made them think that they should go to a lightning strike?"

"Come on, now. Think clearly. It would've taken them longer to come back and switch for veteran jumpers. We both know this last jump was a formality. All four of them were ready to pull numbers for the jump list." He exhaled, clearly frustrated. "I would prefer there were more veterans on this jump, but I'm hoping the fact that they got there faster will offset the lack of experience on the plane."

He was right, of course. She wouldn't have wanted to put anyone's home or lives in danger or risk the fire getting larger because she wasn't ready to see Lance go into danger like this. More, she wasn't prepared yet for the chance she might lose him.

He had been a firefighter for years, but that was before she cared about him. Apparently she could be mad at him, unable to look at him or talk to him, but she still loved him and worried about his safety.

She shook her head, trying to clear that haze. "You're right. Of course. They did the right thing." Was that even her voice? It sounded wrong...off.

"He's good, Meg, you know he is. He's the fastest runner out of the recruit class, faster than anyone on the team save your brothers. And Lizard knew that."

She turned away, because she couldn't argue with that.

She shouldn't even be here. These men had been doing their job for years without her help. She wasn't anything to Lance, no more than she was to any of the other recruits. If Joe wasn't her uncle, would she even have felt comfortable enough to come in here?

"I should go."

"That might be best." The phone next to him rang again. He picked it up and connected, without looking at her. "Buchanan."

She waited, suspended between knowing that she didn't belong and unable to step away, in case there was any news. When Joe's eyes met hers, the grim set of his jaw made her cover her mouth. Something was wrong. "Thanks for letting me know. Keep me informed. I'll make the calls."

Meg didn't even wait for the phone to hit the desk before she leaned forward, asking, "What happened?"

"The house that Will and Lance were protecting…it caved in. Will was inside, and Lance went in to get him. They're waiting."

"My God." Her entire body stilled, paralyzed.

"I've called the hotshots, too. And as soon as Pete and Tim are ready, we'll send the crew back."

"I can go." She couldn't stay here, not when her brother and Lance were potentially hurt.

He shook his head. "We both know you can't." Joe had been there the day she failed so miserably as a firefighter and realized her fear of flames outweighed her need to help others.

"Not as the only medic. I get that. But I'm here." Otherwise, the helplessness would swallow her whole.

"No. That's my final answer. If you want to help, go home and prepare your mother."

The words slammed into her. All she could do was find her mother, tell her that her eldest son was lost in the flames right now.

Along with the man Meg loved.

Nodding, she backed away until she was out of the room. She heard Joe call for her, but she turned and ran, tearing into the parking lot. Having stayed in Bend last night, her bag was still in the car. She jammed the key into the ignition, trying to picture what she would say to her mother. Only then did she realize there were tears streaking down the sides of her face.

* * * *

"Will!" Lance screamed, but his voice was absorbed by the roar of the fire. He scanned the downstairs, or what was left of it. The place wasn't big, but the downstairs was covered with debris, the result of the middle of the house caving in. If the plume of smoke and flames that was pouring out of the house wasn't obstructing his view, he would be able to see into the sky. He had covered his mouth and nose with his face mask, but it was still difficult to breathe.

In the opening into the upstairs, he could see movement…the shapes of two people, one larger than the other.

He needed to get up there. Doing his best to cover his face, he headed toward the stairs to his left. He shoved at some fallen rubble, tossing it out of his path. The top of the stairs, though, was blocked by broken drywall and wreckage. Glancing around, he spotted a splintered two-by-four. He wrenched it from under a bunch of other trash and used it to get a better angle under the stuff in his path.

It was slow going, too slow. Around him, the place continued to burn and the noise and panic blurred in a haze of manic activity.

There were people upstairs who needed help.

After a lifetime, he created enough of an opening to be able to see above him. Will, his face covered in blood and dirt, came into view. "It needs to be bigger," he yelled.

Together, they cleared a larger hole, and Will reached behind him, pulling a girl, no more than eight, covered in grime, from behind his back. She was crying, her hands on her face, and Lance couldn't look at her. Her fear would paralyze him. Will twisted her from above, and Lance attempted to guide her from beneath. It wasn't neat, and every time they accidentally bumped her into something sharp and she cried out, it ripped a piece of his soul away.

Finally, she slipped through. Setting her behind him, he reached for Will. "Come on."

"I'm stuck." Will shook his head. "Get out, with her. I'll get myself clear."

"No. I'm not leaving you." Lance turned to the little girl. "You have to run. Go. Can you do that? Be brave?"

She shook her head. "My mommy..." She pointed upstairs.

Damn it. There was someone else here. "I'll see about your mom. You get to safety." She swiped at her eyes, wavering. Lance pressed the advantage. "Go."

Her panic won out. She turned, scurrying down the stairs and out the door. With her gone, he turned to Will. "I'm coming up."

"Get out of here."

"No." Lance picked up the two-by-four he'd used to make the opening, turning to the hole with more urgency. As he set to work again, the opposite wall of the cabin groaned before crumbling inward.

"Lance, you stubborn fool. Go," Will yelled.

"No." He worked faster, until the hole was big enough for a grown man. Pushing up, he lifted himself. "Where's the girl's mom?"

"Dead."

Lance cursed softly under his breath. Only then did he see Will. "You aren't stuck." He wasn't. Instead, there was a splintered beam through his thigh, too long and bulky to let him escape through the hole he'd made.

"No. I was trying to get you to go."

Why didn't he want him to help him? Did he distrust him that much, that he'd rather take his chances alone and die? "I don't listen to direction well."

Will grimaced. "I know."

Their eyes met and understanding passed between them. "Let's get out of here. I need to get that out of your leg or we can't go."

"I know."

Lance didn't pause, then. He reached down and yanked the splintered beam. As it tore from Will's leg, he screamed. Blood poured from the wound. If they didn't move fast, he'd be yanking Will's body out of this wreckage as he bled out.

Will nodded, significantly paler. With some jostling, they positioned Will at the cleared hole. With a shove, Lance pushed him. Thank God for gravity, because Will burst through the opening with a clumsy tumble, falling down what remained of the stairs. Lance shifted, wiggling himself through and scrambling down to join him. As Will got to his feet, he staggered, met Lance's eyes, and lost consciousness.

Gritting his teeth, Lance grabbed his arm, pulling him up with a burst of energy. Digging his shoulder into Will's armpit, he ignored a stab of pain from his knee, redistributing his weight under his new load. Awkwardly, he dragged both of them toward the door.

There was no warning. A loud crack sounded above him, and he had barely enough time to drop Will to the floor and cover him. What remained of the building crashed down, and the force of the falling wood stole his breath. His ears rang, and his vision clouded, blackening around the edges as he struggled to retain his consciousness. He pushed at the rubbish around him, knowing that if he passed out, he'd die here, in this burning home.

He pulled himself free, reaching for Will. Still out cold, he was dead weight, but Lance managed to loosen the waste of the house from around him.

Unable to bear his weight, he dragged him, under the arms, out the door. On the porch, he threw him over the side, before attempting the stairs. When he failed, his legs giving out from under him, he tumbled down, falling on his face in a heap in the yard.

Through the haze of his blurred vision, he caught sight of four of his teammates. He sighed, giving over to the blackness.

* * * *

Meg and her mother sat in silence in the dirty kitchen at her mom's house, neither looking at each other but unable to be alone. The hum of the refrigerator was the only noise in the kitchen, louder than Meg remembered and grating.

Waiting sucked. Worse than not knowing what happened was the look on her mother's face. There was concern, of course, but also resignation. As if she lived every day in expectation of the call they were waiting for.

Meg had debated driving to the hospital and waiting there, but Joe suggested they sit tight while they waited for news. Her mom's house was between Redmond and Bend. They could easily get to either the air center or the hospital.

After an hour, Meg was crawling out of her skin.

She pushed up, facing the sink. She gripped the counter, but when her knuckles got sore, she forced herself to loosen her fingers. Spinning on her mother, she whispered, "How are you staying so calm? I can't take this."

Her mom flopped back, sighing. "You know, when I met your father, first thing I noticed about him were his eyes. Lots of people say they fall in love with people's eyes, and maybe that's true. Because his eyes..." She grinned. "He had the most sensitive and knowledgeable eyes. Something about them, about how he looked at me, made me feel safe. Our entire lives together, he rarely got angry, always responded thoughtfully. For me, he was the calm in the storm."

She stood, stepping forward to take Meg's hand in her own. Her grip was firm, her palms dry. "He was that force for JT, too. They're right when they say that Lance is just like his father. It's like you can feel the energy under the surface. And while JT needed your father's calm, your father needed his energy."

Meg shook her head. "Why are you telling me this?"

"Because people are who they are. The same thing that made your father a steadying influence in our lives made him a great firefighter. Saving lives, helping others? It was as much a part of him as being your father was." She squeezed Meg's hand. "Those same things drive your brothers...and Lance." Her eyes softened. "Stop trying to make them something they aren't, Meg. Our job isn't to change them. We can only love them as they are."

Meg searched her mother's face. She knew, then, about her feelings for Lance. There was no other explanation. Except, there was no judgment on her features. As if she understood, maybe better even than Meg did. "I'm not sure if I can do this, Mom."

"I know, baby." She wrapped her arms around her daughter. "And know this. We can love them but that doesn't mean we have to love their choices. It's up to you to decide if you can live with them. Because living without them...that can be just as difficult."

Meg's cell phone rang, breaking the tension.

She almost didn't want to answer, but she was stronger than that. She connected, putting it on speakerphone. "Hello?"

"Meg." Mitch sounded serious and grim. "They're at the hospital in Bend. Get there as soon as you can."

"How are they?"

"They are alive." Meg met her mother's eyes, exhaling a breath she didn't realize she was holding. "I'll let the doctors tell you more."

"We're leaving now." They were already out the door.

In the car, Meg met her mother's gaze. There was steel behind her eyes. The past decade had strained what used to be a close relationship between them. Whatever they'd been through, though, Meg was glad her mother was here with her now. She needed her.

Determined to follow her mother's lead, she straightened her shoulders and they headed for Bend.

Chapter 21

Lance came to quietly. He didn't feel right, floating and groggy. His eyelids were heavier than usual, and opening them took herculean effort. When he finally managed to pry them open, his surroundings didn't make sense. There were rails on his bed as well as buzzing and whooshing of machines around him. He lifted his arm to rub his throbbing head, but he couldn't get far thanks to the IV lines attached to his hands and Pulsox on his finger.

He was in the hospital.

Scowling, he tried to piece together what brought him here. The haze was pain medicine.

The fire. The cabin and the girl. The flames and Will. It all rushed back in stops and starts, a cacophony of horror and fear. That's right. They'd almost been killed.

Hell, he had no idea where Will was. All of his hard work keeping him alive had failed.

Maybe he was more like his father that he thought.

Glancing around, he realized he wasn't alone as he originally thought. In the corner, hunched over and looking uncomfortable in a hospital-issue chair, Meg had dozed off, one elbow propped on an armrest, her gorgeous auburn hair spilling out of a ponytail she had long neglected.

As she slept, he was reminded of how incredibly lovely she was. When she was awake, the force of her character was larger than life. Asleep, though, she looked fragile, with her dainty bones and small features. Now, the dark circles under her eyes lent a sense of vulnerability to her as well. How long had he been out? Long enough for her to look tired and too worried.

About him. After all of the things he'd put her through lately. He'd been nothing but heartbreak for her. That ripped at his chest like claws.

"Meg." He didn't want to wake her, but she didn't look comfortable. Besides watching her sleep felt too intimate and he'd given up rights to that a week ago. "Hey. Firecracker. Wake up."

She shifted, wincing. Obviously, her position was worse than he imagined. When her eyes opened, the force of that blue gaze burned him. "You're awake."

"Seems like it. Though I can't be sure, what with all the pain medicine I'm on."

"You're alive."

Her seriousness was unnerving. "I guess so."

She glanced away, sitting up straighter. "It's just...your head. We were waiting for you to wake up. It was touch and go."

Lance knew enough about head trauma to read between the lines. Sometimes, with concussions, people didn't wake up. No explanations, no warning. Just damage to certain spots and presto. Gone.

She'd been sitting there for who knew how long, wondering if he would ever wake up. He allowed the pain and sorrow of that to wash over him as he swallowed, looking down at himself. No obvious casts, so he wiggled his toes. He flexed his hands. All seem to be in working order. There were aches and pains, some worse than others, but he could move everything. "I seem to be okay."

"Nasty gash on your forehead had everyone worried." She motioned toward his leg. "There's bruising on your hip and they were worried about internal damage, but so far so good."

"How's Will?" There was something going on. She was much too serious.

"He's not awake yet. But he's alive. Whatever went through his leg, it missed any major artery, and if it hadn't been for you, he might not have made it out." She bit her lip. "You saved his life."

Gratitude made him uncomfortable. "No problem."

"What happened? They said he went in on his own. If you hadn't followed, he would've been trapped inside." She folded her hands in her lap. "At least that's what the little girl said."

An image of the girl, her dirt-stained face, flashed behind his eyes and he squeezed them closed.

"How is she?" he whispered, having a hard time pretending none of this mattered. His default was bravado, this...it was too much for him.

"She's fine. Said you were the one who got them out. You saved her."

"Yeah, well…if Will had let me go in with him, maybe he wouldn't be in the hospital either."

She cocked her head. "What do you mean?"

"He didn't trust me." Lance shifted, to get more comfortable on the lumpy mattress and maybe avoid the awkward situation. "Refused to take me in to get her, afraid of my decision making, I guess. And who can blame him? I blatantly ignored his directions when I was there."

Her eyes narrowed. "I don't understand."

"In the house. He told me to leave, and I didn't. He lied, said he was stuck. Would have rather taken his chances on his own, but I refused to leave him behind." He shook his head. "I've tried to convince everyone that I'm not reckless, not like my father. But maybe everyone's right. Maybe I am."

"He would be dead. If you listened to him, Will would have died."

"He told me to go because he didn't want to work with me in the first place."

"Lance—"

"Don't. Please. Since I got back no one has trusted me. Not all the way. Maybe with good reason." He shook his head. "I couldn't leave him in there, though. You understand, don't you?" He searched her face, afraid that he might find judgment there. It had been an impossible decision. Will might have wanted him to go, but he wouldn't have been able to live with himself if he hadn't done everything in his power to save him.

"No one expected you to leave him."

"Will did." Had Will really been willing to die instead of accepting his help? "No matter what I do, or maybe because of the things I do, no one is ever going to trust me here." He met her troubled blue eyes. "Come on. I even lied to you."

She didn't pretend or offer any false disagreement, because they both knew he was right. He kept so many secrets and now in the face of the truth about his father, that it had all been for nothing, that was what he regretted the most: lying to her.

It had all seemed worth it, before. Back when he believed his cause was righteous, that he would be vindicated when the truth was out. He'd convinced himself that she would understand. Of all his mistakes, that had been the most reckless thing he'd done.

"I'm going to go along with a transfer. I think Bates and Joe are right. There's nothing here for me. Team requires trust and I've lost that."

"You could fix that. You could explain yourself. You could apologize." She stood up, her spine straight and her eyes broken. "You could stay and fight for me. For us. For what you're doing here."

"You know it won't work. No one sees me as anything more than his son, just as irresponsible. I'll never be anything else." Even considering that he would be in a situation again like this one, with Will not having any faith in him…it couldn't happen. It wouldn't.

"I never saw you like that." Her voice was soft, but it didn't conceal how much she was hurting. All he ever seemed to do was hurt her.

But it was so clear. He couldn't stay in Redmond this way. Someone had been trying to hurt him, and if it wasn't because he was trying to find information about his father, then it was because they didn't want him here. Someone hated him enough to harm him. He wouldn't stay in Redmond and put Meg or any of his teammates in any more danger.

What happened with Will exposed exactly how much suspicion of him still existed. If the team didn't believe in him, he couldn't work with them.

And he was definitely having some difficulty believing in himself.

"This is for the best." The words choked him. Watching her absorb them, it was daggers in his gut. He swung his legs over the edge of the bed, shifting to stand, and gasped as pain radiated up his spine. He gritted his teeth, forcing himself to take it.

He should have never returned here, to Redmond.

He held his arm out. "Can you remove these IVs for me? I need to get out of here."

"You don't want people to think you make reckless decisions? Then make a smart one and stay." She stood, her back stiff and straight. He could see the pain in her, but her anger was stronger. "Besides, you're plenty capable of running away without my help."

Turning on her heel, she swept from his hospital room. From his perch on the side of his bed, he watched her go.

Was he running? He buried his face in his hands. No, that wasn't what this was. He was accepting reality.

This wasn't the place for him.

* * * *

After leaving Lance's room, Meg crept in to Will's. Her mom sat next to him, clinging to his free hand.

"Second time in less than a month I'm holding the hand of my unconscious son in the hospital. Different son, different bed, but the same helplessness."

Meg stepped next to her, dropping her hand on her shoulder. "Why don't you go get something to eat?"

"I'm not hungry."

"You haven't eaten all day, Mom. Go. I'll stay here with him." She didn't want to tell her mother that she would prefer to be alone, but it would be easier to recover herself if she wasn't around.

Her mom must've seen something on her face, because she nodded, getting to her feet. "I suppose I could take a break. I'll be back." She paused, looking over her daughter. "I'll bring you some food, too."

Her mother squeezed her arms as she walked out, vacating her seat. Meg took up sentry duty, reaching for Will's hand. "Wake up."

"I'm here." Her brother's voice was raspy, probably the result of the air tube they'd removed earlier or not having eaten anything or drunk anything in forty-eight hours.

She shot out of her seat. "My God, you're awake."

"The girl, the girl." His eyes were hazy, and she wasn't sure if he even knew what he was talking about.

"She's fine. You guys got hurt." She hoped he couldn't hear how heartsick her voice was, but the effort to hold back tears right now was more difficult than she expected.

"Lance…"

"He's fine, too."

"His fault…all his."

"What are you talking about?" From every account, Lance had been a hero on that mountain. When her brother didn't answer, she debated waiting, asking him later. She shouldn't push him too hard, not in his condition. But she needed to hear. Had to understand what he was saying. She shook his hand. "Will. What do you mean?"

"Shouldn't have come." His voice was barely above a whisper, and she leaned forward to hear better.

"To the cabin?" Did he mean that Lance shouldn't have followed him in to help the girl? That's what Lance had said, that Will hadn't wanted him there, hadn't trusted him.

"To Redmond. Should have stayed gone." His eyes found hers briefly, but they weren't focused. Maybe this was the drugs talking. He might not even realize who he was talking to.

"He saved your life."

"Doesn't make up for killing our father."

"He didn't do that. That was his father."

"Only a matter of time before he makes that kind of mistake, too. I tried to get him to leave. So stubborn."

Meg's stomach dropped. Her throat tightened, and the tears she had barely been holding in trickled from her eyes. No, this couldn't be. "Will, no…"

"The parachute. The sand. Didn't want to hurt him, only wanted him to go."

She shook her head, stifled a sob. Her brother, someone she had grown up with, her family. "No, it can't be…"

This time, when he turned his head and met her eyes, she could see her brother. He might be drugged up, but he was telling the truth. "Joe needs to know. Maybe, maybe it will be enough to make him leave anyway. I can't keep it to myself anymore." He swallowed with difficulty. "I didn't want him to stay in the burning house because I can't live with what I've done anymore. Can't live with myself. It would have been better if I'd died."

He'd meant to die there, wanted to?

Meg pulled her fingers from his hand. "I'm in love with him. You knew how I felt about him."

"I'm sorry. For that, I am sorry. But not for trying to save the rest of us. Not for that."

She pushed back in her chair. "Will, how could you? You could have killed someone."

A tear trickled out of her brother's eye, but he didn't respond.

"You're sick." There was no explanation. Her brother had changed irrevocably after their father died and somewhere along the line, he'd begun to suffer. But she'd had no idea that his pain had transformed into this single-minded hatred. Staring at him, listening to the fervor as he explained the things he'd done…something in him was broken and he needed help.

Still…she couldn't look at him now, and there weren't any words that would patch things. This was a level of horror she didn't understand and refused to accept. She'd go to the air center now, to tell Joe and Bates, get the proper authorities involved. This couldn't wait.

Standing, she gazed down at her brother's broken form. He wasn't going anywhere soon. This hospital bed could be his prison for now.

She had no idea if she would ever get over this, if she would ever be able to look at her brother without seeing someone who would risk another person's life. All she wanted to do right now was get away from him. "Goodbye, Will. Be well."

In the hall, she leaned against the wall, her head falling backwards until it smacked the cinderblock behind her. She needed to tell Joe. She had to tell them right now. Her own brother…it was so impossible, except it wasn't. She knew Will was angry, and she hadn't been able to get through to him. None of them had.

"Meg?" Her mother's voice broke her out of her daze.

She pushed away from the wall, turning to face her mother and attempting a smile. This wasn't the time, not to break her mother's heart. Not with him in a hospital bed. There would be time for that in the days to come.

"I need to get back to the air center. I forgot to do some paperwork for the end of rookie training."

Her mother's eyes narrowed. "Right now? I'm sure Uncle Joe would understand."

"Yes, right now." She clutched her handbag closer to her side, using a steely grip to focus her energy.

Her mother sighed. "Well, then, if you have to go, you have to go."

Meg folded her mother into a tight squeeze. She dropped her face into the crease of her mother's neck, closing her eyes and breathing in deeply. How were they ever going to get through this?

That was a question for another day. Today, though, she could do this. She could tell Joe, and she could do the right thing.

She pulled away from her mother, holding her at arm's length. "I'll be home tonight."

Her mom nodded. "Drive safe. I can't do this anymore." When Meg cocked her head in question, her mother glanced toward Will's room. "Sit by another hospital bed."

Meg couldn't respond around the lump in her throat, so she offered a sick smile and left.

Checking her watch, she realized it was close to six o'clock. Joe might not be there, but she hoped he was finishing up paperwork. She slipped into the elevator, determined to do the right thing.

Chapter 22

"Borrowing Sledge's truck to come get you?" Dak grumbled, his hands tucked into the pocket of his cargo shorts. "That guy's going to remind me forever that I owe him one."

"Thanks." Now that Lance was up and moving, all the aches and pains he'd been ignoring earlier decided to scream. "I appreciate it."

Dak shrugged. He hit the lock on Sledge's key fob, and the truck beeped its alarm in the parking lot of the air center. "How you feeling, now?"

"Everything hurts."

"Think we passed our final jump test, though, don't you?"

"Yeah." He let out a mirthless laugh. They were official. A few more days in the building, but it was a formality, really. Smokejumpers. This was everything he'd ever wanted. He'd been training for this, sweating and working for it for years. Now that the moment had arrived, he'd expected it to be filled with triumph. He'd proved to the world that he wasn't his father.

Except that wasn't what was singing through him. With Will in the hospital, the result of not wanting to work beside him, with someone still on the loose who wanted to hurt him, this milestone was overshadowed by fear and disappointment.

"I'm going to request a transfer."

"What?" Dak pulled to a stop next to him, snagging his sleeve. "What the hell are you talking about?"

"Come on. You've been here. You can see what a disaster this has been. Someone's sabotaging my stuff, my truck. They almost got Hunter killed with that parachute stunt. And now? Will doesn't even want to work with me." He buried his hands in his hair. "This was a bad idea. I shouldn't have come back here."

"Holy drama."

The comment stopped Lance short. "What does that mean?"

"This." Dak waved over him, amusement on his face. "You're acting as if you thought this would be easy."

Lance could only stare at him.

"You planned to come in here like a conquering hero. All, my father was wrongfully accused, and look at how amazing of a firefighter I've become. And, a little bit of, this town abandoned me, but I still succeeded." He chuckled. "But the truth is, shit like this is hard. People don't want to be proved wrong. They want to be proved right. Now that you've found some resistance, you're ready to turn tail and run." His face sobered. "I never figured you for a quitter."

The words were harsh, and so much harder than anything he expected out of his friend. "You don't understand."

"I do. I've been watching you search for information. I've watched you hold yourself away from the rest of the team. I thought I was the distant and brooding one. You had me beat."

"That's not what I was doing. They're the ones who were judging me."

"Please." Dak snorted. "Get over yourself. You expected them to snub you."

"That's not true."

"Things are hard, but I never pinpointed you as the sort to run away." Dak paused. "Like what you're doing with Meg Buchanan."

"I'm not running away." Even as he said the words, he couldn't deny he'd thought this would be easier.

"You're going to leave here, let whatever dickhead's trying to scare you win. That's what you're doing." Dak put his hands on his hips. "Mostly, though, you're going to leave the woman you love behind because you're too afraid to let her down."

"You've gone too far."

"I should have gone further before." He stepped forward. Though his words caused Lance's chest to hurt, he didn't find any anger in his friend's face, only sympathy and concern. "I'm your friend and I love you, man. But you need to take a hard look at what it is that you want. I thought you wanted to come home, to prove you were your own man. Not only that you weren't your father, but that you made your own choices and lived your own life. If you are, then show them that. You're too caught up in what they think. Show them what you think. Show them who you are. And have some faith."

Dak stepped back, then, and turned toward the air center, leaving Lance alone with the havoc he'd wreaked.

Is that what this was? Had he expected this to be easy? In his soul, he'd never believed his father would put anyone at risk without a good reason. But that didn't mean everyone else felt the same way.

Was he too caught up on how the rest of the town viewed him?

Meg's face played across his mind. He closed his eyes, inhaling through the pain. He'd convinced himself that he'd lost her because of the circumstances. If he had to admit that he lost her because of his own choices…

The agony tore at his chest.

Maybe this wasn't a good idea. Meg had said as much, that he was running instead of staying and standing his ground, helping to find whoever was trying to hurt him. Someone at the base was threatening him. Would he leave here and allow that person to remain?

Was his ego worth giving up Meg? His brain offered him the future without her. Of never seeing her smile, of never watching the flush rise in her cheeks when he pushed her buttons.

He would never be able to touch her again.

No. Absolutely not.

God, he'd been so stupid. He had wanted her his entire life. Yet he'd thrown that away because the town didn't see him the way he hoped. He'd been ashamed, and his ego had taken a hit. Is that what had kept him from standing and fighting?

That's not who he wanted to be. That's definitely not the man Meg deserved.

Decided, he strode toward Joe Buchanan's office. He'd tell him right now that he wasn't going anywhere. That he'd do whatever he had to do to find the person threatening him, and that he deserved the chance to follow his family legacy here.

Then, he'd beg Meg for forgiveness and hope she was willing to give it to him.

Except Joe's office was dark. Where had he gone? He wouldn't know that Lance was out of the hospital, and Will was still there. If he wasn't here, maybe he was at the hospital.

He sauntered to the desk, scanning it absently.

Usually, it was covered in paperwork. Today, there was only a note on it. He didn't mean to read it, but it was there.

It was short, but by the end, his heart had kicked up. He rushed out of the room, hurrying to the barracks and Dak. When he found him, his friend was taking off his shoes, getting comfortable.

"We need to go," he said. "Joe's in danger."

* * * *

Meg tried to call Joe twice on her ride to the air center, but he didn't pick up. When she arrived, the place was teeming with Forest Service personnel, but Joe's office was dark. According to one of the other administrators, Joe left for the hospital over an hour earlier to see Will and Lance, but Meg knew that wasn't true. She'd come from there, and she would have seen him. An hour was plenty of time to get to Bend.

In the parking lot, she tried calling him again, but she went to voicemail once more. Where the hell was he? Now wasn't the time for him to go missing, not after Will and Lance were hurt. Something was wrong.

Meg dialed her mother. When she picked up, she asked, "Is Joe there?"

"No. Why?"

"They told me he was on his way to the hospital." Meg pressed her palm against her forehead. "Don't worry. I'm going to find him." She said goodbye, and hung up. She glared at her phone. Where would he go?

He'd been working hard. Maybe he'd gone home, to get something before he went to the hospital to see her family. Decided, she got back in her car and drove the short distance to her uncle's apartment. His truck was parked out front, and she sighed with relief. After everything that had happened to Lance, she'd been worried.

She texted her mother that she had found him as she walked to ring the bell.

No answer. She knocked, texting her uncle again. He had to be inside. Her anxiety ratcheted up, and she started banging on the door, calling for him, "Joe. Are you in there?"

The door opened, like the last person in hadn't closed it all the way. That was strange. The hair on her neck tingled. She pushed forward, stepping into her uncle's foyer. "Hello?"

Maybe something had happened to him. He could have fallen, hit his head. He wasn't a young man, and he didn't always eat right. With visions of cardiac and stroke victims swirling in her head, she hurried forward, finding the living room and kitchen empty. She pushed open the door to the bedroom. While she had been entertaining thoughts of him unconscious from stroke or heart attack, what she found was even more chilling.

Her uncle sat on the edge of his bed, a pistol in his hand. His elbows were propped on his knees, and the gun rested, currently pointed at the ground. Meg stopped short. "Uncle Joe?"

He shook his head slowly, moving the gun from one hand to the other between his knees. "Meggy, you shouldn't have come here."

"What is this? What's going on?" She remained just inside the doorway, not wanting to spook him by getting any closer.

"This isn't how I hoped it would happen." His voice was soft, but it rang with defeat.

"What happened?" She lifted her hands, not wanting to appear threatening. Her uncle's mind wasn't a healthy space. Her gaze dropped to the pistol. "Why don't you put the gun down? We can talk about this."

"I haven't said anything for ten years. I doubt talking is going to fix it now."

"I don't understand." She needed to keep up the conversation. It was the only way she might be able to defuse this. She didn't know much about suicide situations, so her best bet was to buy some time.

"I thought if Lance came back, if he got another chance, it would help right the wrongs I did back then." He exhaled, his shoulders slumping forward further. "But everything has only gotten worse. So much worse."

"What wrongs are you trying to right, Uncle Joe?" There was something larger here, something she didn't understand.

"It was my fault. Your father, Lance's father…they're dead because of me."

She shook her head. "No. The tapes…JT convinced Dad to go—"

"Because of me." Joe lifted his gaze, suddenly angry. He got to his feet, coming toward her, gun still in his hand. It remained pointed toward the ground, but she backed away. Joe's state of mind was not good, and she didn't trust him right now. He continued, his voice sharp and bitter. "I jumped first. I had an anxiety attack in the air, and steered wrong. I don't know how it happened, now, looking back…but Lance's dad…he saw me. It takes…I've heard the tapes. He was convincing my brother, your dad to come after me." He shook his head. "If they hadn't, I would've died."

Meg ran through what she remembered of the tape, trying to piece together what she had heard with what her uncle was telling her. "Are you saying that JT convinced my father to help you?"

"Your father, my brother…he knew it was dangerous. JT also knew that if Jason had let me go, he would have never been able to forgive himself for letting me die. JT tried to save your father from a lifetime of regrets."

"They were trying to save you." All of it made more sense knowing why they jumped. But that didn't answer the greater question. "You told everyone that it was an accident that got you all on the wrong side. But it was your fault they were dead? There's more to the story, isn't there? What happened?"

According to the files, JT and her father had continued to fight the fire even after it became clear that it was too dangerous. "You told the inspectors that Lance's dad and mine stayed too long because they were arrogant. What are you not telling us?"

Joe sat down and buried his face in his hands. "I panicked. I messed up, and when I was on the ground, I panicked. I ran, and my shelter was lost. Your father came after me." He looked up at her, eyes pleading. "I took your father's shelter. I ran away with his shelter because I had lost mine and I left your father behind."

She covered her mouth, unable to breathe through the pain of it. "No...Uncle Joe..."

"I didn't know that he was going to die, Meggy. They were more seasoned than I was. I figured they'd read it all better than I could, that they would find their way out. But they didn't." He swallowed a sob. "I didn't want to die."

"They didn't want to die either."

She should be afraid. He had a gun. Provoking someone in such distress wasn't smart. But her anger was a fierce pit in her stomach. "That was your brother. And you were careless, and even if you didn't mean to get him killed, he's dead. And you're alive. I've grown up without a father, and Lance grew up thinking it was his father's fault, when he was actually a hero and trying to save you."

Joe lurched to his feet, his face twisted into a mask of despair. "Don't you think I know that? I spent every day over the last ten years beating myself up about what I could have done differently. About all of the mistakes I made." He waved the gun around in agitation.

Meg sobered. She shouldn't have upset him.

"I thought if I could make it up to Lance, I could undo some of the harm I've done."

"Why don't you put the gun down?" He was obviously in turmoil, and her fear ratcheted up. "We can talk about this more then."

Joe's eyes fell on the weapon in his hand, as if only remembering he was carrying it. He swallowed, his fingers tightening around the butt of the pistol. Meg waited, not wanting to tempt fate, hoping the uncle she'd loved all these years would make the right decision.

His arm straightened, lifting the pistol and training it on her. "No more talking. This ends tonight. I've kept this secret all these years. It will die with us."

Chapter 23

Lance counted the seconds for the police to arrive and prayed they wouldn't be too late. Until then, he and Dak had taken up positions outside.

He'd seen Meg's Pathfinder. She was inside, with Joe.

They'd hoped they could talk to Joe, convince him that whatever plans he'd had to take his own life were unnecessary, that there were people who cared about him. They were going to appeal to his love of family, to the good he did at the air center. They'd discussed it on the drive, come up with a plan. Dak had called 911 on their way.

Nothing had prepared them for the situation spinning out of control in front of them.

Discovering Meg here had chilled him to the bones, made the stakes even higher.

As they listened to Joe's story, waiting for a moment to intervene safely, the disjointed and manic way he relayed the details sent his fear into overdrive. Joe was obviously unstable, and there was no telling what he was capable of. The horror of this situation, of what he'd said, had filled Lance with numb betrayal. Joe...he would have never expected it. But nothing—none of his shock or anger—could compare with the terrible icy panic of knowing Meg was in his crosshairs right now and having so few options to help her.

God, please, let him not touch a hair on her precious head.

Paralyzed, he listened as she tried to talk him down. She sounded so rational and calm. If he and Dak went in, they might spook him and give him a reason to use the gun he obviously had.

Every second he left her in there, alone, ate at his gut in a way he couldn't explain, was powerless against.

"No more talking. This ends tonight, and I've kept this secret all these years. It will die with us."

No.

Lance was up, running, before he could look at Dak. He needed to get to her, had to put himself between Meg and her uncle.

He collided with Meg in the living room. The relief was a warm wave as he shifted her behind him in time to confront Joe as he rushed out of his bedroom.

Joe would need to go through him if he wanted to get to her. The rightness of that filled his chest, relief singing through him.

He lifted his hand, doing his best to conceal Meg as completely as he could behind him, protecting her. "Joe. Please listen."

"Get out of the way, Roberts." Joe's hand shook, the gun trembling precariously.

"No. I know what happened. Dak's outside, too. We heard everything. There's no way to hide now. Killing Meg won't change that." He stepped closer, making himself a bigger target, distracting him from Meg. "You don't want to kill her. She's your niece, you love her."

"You don't know anything." His scream was unhinged, full of desperation and panic.

"I do. I know how you stole your own brother's shelter to save your life, leaving my father and Jason to their deaths. I heard it all." It was nearly impossible to contain his anger, but he tried.

Joe covered his eyes with his palm, the gun still in his hand. "Oh, God. That's true. That's exactly what I did."

Still holding his hand between him and Joe, with Meg behind him, Lance attempted to rein in the situation, at least until she was safe. He needed to keep him talking, distracted and off-kilter. "Joe. This isn't what Jason would want, for you to threaten his only daughter. This isn't what you want to do."

"It's my fault, that Will was targeting you. You don't know how many times I wanted to tell him that he had it all wrong."

"Will?" This couldn't be. Will was angry, of course, but not enough to threaten him. And the parachute...Hunter...

"After Hunter got hurt, I told him to stop, that someone was going to get killed. He wouldn't listen to me. Nothing I said would help you. Hunter...that's my fault. All of this is my fault." His voice trailed off, hopeless and empty.

.

"Put the gun down, Joe." The faint sound of sirens split the air. "We'll talk to the police and the Forest Services. We'll talk to them, explain everything. Whatever you're thinking doesn't have to happen."

"It's too late now." Joe turned, and Lance caught the faint movement as he lifted the pistol to his chin.

"No," he shouted, lunging forward. "Joe, no!"

Except the gun went off, and the base manager fell to the floor.

* * * *

Representatives from the coroner's office came to collect the body, gathering evidence and taking statements. Meg recited the entire ordeal matter-of-factly, as if it was a movie she'd watched or an event that had happened to someone else. Lance had stood next to her, holding her hand. She allowed him to do it because she needed to touch someone right now. The coldness that had settled inside her after her experience with her uncle had shaken her, left her wondering if anything made sense anymore.

First Will's confession that he'd done things that put both Hunter and Lance's lives in jeopardy. Finding Joe, hearing his story? That would have been bad enough, added cracks to her already shaken world. But to have him threaten her?

She was equal parts broken and relieved to be alive and she didn't know how to process that.

It was as if her entire world had crumbled around her tonight. She had no idea how she was going to tell her mother about any of this.

As soon as the officials finished talking with Lance, he drove her back to Bend, as if he sensed that she needed to get away from all of this. He promised to bring her back tomorrow to pick up her car. Besides, she didn't know if she could drive right now.

Her uncle was dead.

Wordlessly, Lance walked her upstairs to her apartment and unlocked the door for her. She followed him inside, standing in the middle of the room, directionless.

"Meg..." He stepped forward, taking her hand again. Like before, she let him.

"I'm not sure I want to talk, Lance." She had no idea what he had to say, but she'd prefer to stay here with him tracing circles into the back of her hand until the world faded away.

"I know. But, I have to."

Here it came. The great Lance Roberts escape plan. She pulled her fingers from his, shifting away from him. "You don't have to do this. I get it. I'll even say it all for you. You don't feel like anyone is ever going to accept you. What could have happened to me..." She waved her arm in an arch. "Proof that you shouldn't be here. That the past is still in our present."

"No problem. I get it." She swallowed. "Thanks for the ride. I really appreciate it." Sweeping away from him, she headed toward the kitchen. She needed some space.

As she reached for a mug, determined to make tea, anything to occupy her hands, he caught her arm, stopping her. "Whoa. That's not what I was going to say at all." He reached forward, grasping her and pulling her closer.

She didn't want to look at him, didn't want to see whatever she would find in his eyes. The truth was she couldn't handle losing anyone else, not tonight. Maybe tomorrow she'd be stronger, but tonight? She would crumble into a million pieces.

"I'm sorry."

Glancing up, she did her best to remain closed off. She'd never managed to do that before where Lance was concerned, though, and she didn't now.

He squeezed her arms. "I'm so sorry, Meg. I let you down."

Closing her eyes, she bit her lips hard, trying to keep from hearing or seeing anything that would weaken her further. But his voice...God, his voice. She couldn't escape it.

"You were right. I was running away. When I came back to Redmond, I had these grand plans to prove to everyone that they had me and my family all wrong. That my father wasn't as they remembered, as they tried to convince me to remember. More, I wasn't what they would have me be." He shook his head. "It mattered so much, proving myself, that I kept secrets from you, the person I loved the most. When I realized I was falling for you, I should have told you exactly what I was doing. Hell, I should have told you right away. You deserved the truth. Except I was afraid you'd be the one to see through me. What if I wasn't that different from my father? What if I was exactly what I always feared I was?"

He inhaled, replenishing his breath. "And you know what? They're right. I'm a whole lot more like my father than I ever wanted to admit. But I don't care. My father was the sort of man who would sacrifice everything for his friends and family. That's something I understand. I would like to think that I would be strong enough to do the same."

His voice broke on the end, and she couldn't remain still. She reached up, wrapping her arms around his neck. The words wouldn't come, the words he needed to hear, because if she started talking, she'd fall apart. But she could hold him.

He tilted his face, dropping it into the curve of her neck. The next words were whispered, but they rang with sincerity. "I love you, Meg. I've loved you my entire life. I don't want to be the sort of man who doesn't stand by the people he loves. I don't want to be the sort of man who wouldn't stay here, in Redmond, and fight for you. And if that makes me like my father, so be it."

She laughed, then, and the sound was soaked in tears. "You want to stay here? With me?"

"I love you. Will you give me a chance?" He lowered his forehead, touching it to hers. "I promise that I'll never let you down, not ever again." He met her eyes, his gaze suddenly fierce. "And I swear to you, I will always do everything in my power to come home to you, if you'll have me."

It was more than she'd ever hoped for.

"Yes, just yes. I love you, too, Lance." Because she would rather shoulder the uncertainty of loving this man than live the rest of her life without him.

He searched her face, his eyes full of softness and humility…and love.

Reaching up, she cupped his face in her hands. Pulling him closer, she planted her lips on his.

He didn't need any encouragement. Tugging her forward, he captured her mouth. She tangled her fingers into the hair at his nape and closed her eyes, allowing herself the joy of falling into him.

She knew that all of the risks of loving him remained. He was still a firefighter and tomorrow, he could go back up in a plane and jump into the most dangerous situation in the world.

But tonight—forever—he was hers.

"Yes," she said, when she finally surfaced from the drugged experience of kissing him. "Yes."

* * * *

Training stopped for a week after Joe died. Investigators came in, talked to everyone, and that decade-long chapter finally came to a close.

Meg spent the hiatus with her mother, and they quietly buried Joe next to his brother in the family plot.

When training resumed, things were different at the air center. With Joe gone, Mitch stepped into his role as base manager until the Forest Services could finish their investigations and decide what would happen next. Many at the base hoped they'd let Mitch stay on. His days as a trainer might be over, but he was an asset and understood the workings of the place better than anyone else.

A week after they buried Joe, with training completed, the remaining four smokejumper recruits—Lance, Dak, Sledge, and Rock—were added to the jump list. There hadn't been any fire calls yet, but the season would begin soon enough.

Meg wasn't sure what her future at the air center held, but one thing was certain: as of the end of training, she wasn't currently employed there. Therefore, there was no issue inviting the new jumpers for dinner at her mother's place the following week. Or revealing that she and Lance were involved.

So, when they pulled up in Sledge's truck and her eyes found Lance, she didn't hesitate as she swept off the porch and threw herself into his arms.

He laughed as he caught her against him, burying his face in her neck. "Hey you."

"Hey yourself."

Behind her, someone cleared their throat. She pulled back and turned to find Rock rubbing the back of his neck. "I'll take one of those congratulatory hugs, if you're handing them out."

"Fat chance, Rock," Lance said, tucking her into his side. "She reserves those for me."

"Bummer. You really are a buzzkill, Roberts."

She laughed, stepping away and giving the other three jumpers quicker, friendly squeezes, too. "Congratulations, you guys. Come on in. I made Italian."

As they filed inside, Meg still couldn't get over the changes in her mother's house. Unlike the days after Meg's father died, she hadn't been the only one who'd needed the distraction of cleaning and cooking. Her mother had joined her this time. The result was a huge improvement to the state of their living arrangements.

But it had definitely been a rough few weeks. At first, Meg had been worried that her mother would retreat further into herself, that she might be lost for good this time.

Instead, it was as if finding out the truth had brought her old mom back from wherever she'd been hiding. She hadn't talked much, but she'd been present and solid.

Sometimes, that's the best anyone could expect.

Over the past weeks, the authorities had agreed with Will's doctors, that he should be moved to a medical facility that would get him both physical and psychiatric care. They still didn't know what sort of legal repercussions he would face, but the future would need to wait. At least until they could determine the extent of his mental and physical ailments.

What would come next was a long process of healing. But, this time, Meg was confident her mom would stay with her. That they would do it together.

As they went inside, Hunter waited, propped in a wheelchair with his leg and arm in full casts. He was strung as tight as a bow.

It was him that she worried about the most. She had no idea where his head was these days, but it wasn't good. Though she'd tried to talk to him, he refused to open up. Who could blame him? Not only was he working through Joe and his betrayals, but Will, his own brother, was responsible for his injuries, injuries that might end his firefighting career. Of course, he would be in a strange place.

Somehow, they would need to break through to him. Will had buried his pain and they would be dealing with that fallout for the rest of their lives. She refused to repeat history.

Lance had tried to call Hunter, but he hadn't returned any messages. She hoped if they could spend some more time together...

The room quieted, when his fellow recruits saw Hunter. Finally, though, he offered them all a wry grin. "Congratulations, you assholes."

Everyone seemed to take a collective breath as they chuckled.

"Don't think those wheels are going to keep you out of this job, Buchanan. I expect to see you back at training in the spring." Rock crossed his arms over his chest. "You're a glutton for punishment, like the rest of us."

"Damn right. And you can count on it." Seeing the glint in his eyes, the determination...it gave her hope.

"Good, man." Rock stepped forward, clasping Hunter on the shoulder. "Good to see you."

Her mom stepped in from the kitchen, then, dispelling any remaining tension. "Food's ready. Let's eat."

They all chatted and ribbed each other, filing into the dining room. She stepped behind Hunter's wheelchair, waiting to maneuver him in.

Her brother snagged Lance's sleeve and waited until everyone else was out of ear shot. Then he said, "I just wanted to tell you"—he glanced up at Meg—"both of you, actually, that I'm happy for you."

He grinned, though there were shadows in his eyes. "I'm sorry, too. That I didn't give you a better chance, in the beginning. I should have intervened, with Will. I listened to him rant about you all the time, and I said nothing. Maybe if I had..."

Listening to her brother's guilt hurt her in the place that was still raw. How long would healing take?

"It's forgotten." Lance held out his hand. "I'm glad you're healing up."

Hunter nodded, and she gazed at Lance, allowing all of the love inside her to shine through. He winked.

To dispel any awkwardness, she pushed Hunter's chair into the dining room, and set him up next to the rest of the guys. As the good-natured ribbing continued, she took a moment to glance around the table and feel thankful. There may be signs of strain on her mother's face, circles under her eyes. But she was trying to smile. Her brother, too. It would take time, but they would work through this.

Beside her, Lance squeezed her fingers, and she glanced up at him. Though they didn't speak, his eyes said everything she needed to hear.

He was there. And he wasn't going anywhere.

She squeezed back.

Meet the Author

Award winning author and RITA® finalist Marnee Blake used to teach high school students but these days she only has to wrangle her own children. Originally from a small town in Western Pennsylvania, she now battles traffic in southern New Jersey where she lives with her hero husband and their happily ever after: two very energetic boys. When she isn't writing, she can be found refereeing disputes between her children, cooking up something sweet, or hiding from encroaching dust bunnies with a book.

Stay connected with Marnee by signing up for her newsletter at: http://www.subscribepage.com/marneeblake.

Find Marnee on the web at www.marneeblake.com, on Twitter @ marneeblake, or on Facebook at www.facebook.com/AuthorMarneeBlake/.

Acknowledgments

First, so many thanks to you, dear reader, for giving my smokejumpers a chance. I wouldn't be able to do this job without you. Also, a huge thank you to my amazing editor, Esi Sogah, and to my super-agent, Helen Breitwieser. This book wouldn't be what it is without your guidance and support.

Finally, to my husband and our boys… I love you all. Thanks for sharing me with the people I make up in my head.

Keep an eye out for more from
The SmokeJumpers series

Coming soon
From
Marnee Blake
And
Lyrical Liaison